"After all these years of knowing each other, I feel like I'm only now getting to know the real you."

"That could be dangerous."

"It is. But not for the reasons you might think," Katie admitted softly. Cupping his chin in her hands, she kissed him slowly, with a tenderness that melted the edges of the iceberg that had lodged itself in his heart so long ago he couldn't remember when it hadn't been there.

Blake wrapped his arms around her and matched her kiss as moonlight drenched them in a soft glow. Pliable and willing, she melded to his chest, her supple body inviting him to touch. Sliding his hands down her back, he nudged her closer, and when she responded, he deepened their kiss….

Dear Reader,

Taking on new challenges is sometimes frightening, always thrilling, hopefully rewarding. Such was the case when we were given the privilege of collaborating with other Special Edition authors on THE FOLEYS AND THE McCORDS series. Writing as partners, our twosome suddenly became a "sevensome" to develop this series. It stretched our skills and gave us a backstage look at how our fellow authors create.

The Texas CEO's Secret was—in short—a blast to write. Watching as the touching complexity of the love affair between Katie Whitcomb-Salgar and Blake McCord developed, we found our own emotions entrenched in their lives and in the lives of the other Foleys and McCords.

That's the fun thing about writing and reading romance—living vicariously through characters who, simply put, are merely people like us, with the same loves, losses, joys, sorrows, dreams, hopes and fears we all have.

It is with this thought in mind we hope you enjoy the exciting, passionate unfolding of Blake and Katie's discovery that they are meant for each other.

Nicole Foster

THE TEXAS CEO'S SECRET

NICOLE FOSTER

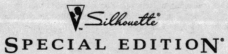

SPECIAL EDITION

Published by Silhouette Books

America's Publisher of Contemporary Romance

Special thanks and acknowledgment
to Nicole Foster for her contribution to
The Foleys and the McCords miniseries.

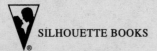

SILHOUETTE BOOKS

ISBN-13: 978-0-373-65485-7

PLEASE RECYCLE
THIS PRODUCT IS RECYCLABLE

Recycling programs
for this product may
not exist in your area.

THE TEXAS CEO'S SECRET

Visit Silhouette Books at www.eHarlequin.com

Printed in U.S.A.

NICOLE FOSTER

is the pseudonym for the writing team of Danette Fertig-Thompson and Annette Chartier-Warren. Both journalists, they met while working on the same newspaper, and started writing historical romance together after discovering a shared love of the Old West and happy endings. Their twenty-year friendship has endured writer's block, numerous caffeine-and-chocolate deadlines, and the joyous chaos of marriage and raising five children between them. They love to hear from readers. Send a SASE for a bookmark to PMB 228, 8816 Manchester Rd., Brentwood, MO 63144.

For my partner.

In all our years collaborating as partners,
friends and sisters, writing this book was
a unique experience. For us to be able to share it
made it the best experience possible. Thanks, partner.

Chapter One

It was a lover's night, velvet-dark and sultry, with silvered moonlight and the intimacy of midnight stillness that invited temptation and seduction.

But Katerina Whitcomb-Salgar wasn't with the man she'd professed to love and had intended to marry. She'd left him behind, another woman in his arms, along with the confidence that there were certainties she could rely on, and at the top of the list was that one day she'd be Mrs. Tate McCord.

Instead, she was on her way home with Tate's older brother and wondering what the lingering revelers at the party they'd abandoned were making of that. More strongly, she questioned herself and what had prompted her to accept his unexpected invitation to escort her to her doorstep.

Katie looked sidelong at Blake McCord, covertly

studying his profile in the dim shifting glow of passing cars and streetlights. He and his brother shared the same dark blond good looks, but Blake's arrogance and focused resolve, the qualities she'd defined him by over the years, showed clearly in the lean, hard lines of his features. He and Tate were so different, almost opposites; nothing about him should have attracted her.

Yet here she was, alone with him and conscious of an edgy, almost nervous energy that was both unfamiliar and unsettling.

"You're very quiet," he said, in a low voice that filled the silence in the car and betrayed no emotion except polite concern.

"I'm sorry, it's been a long evening." It had nearly been an evening at home. She'd considered making her excuses about attending the lavish Labor Day party at the McCords' Dallas mansion, especially days after she and Tate had broken their engagement, knowing people would be talking, speculating, asking questions. But backing out simply to avoid a few uncomfortable hours seemed cowardly so she'd put on a little black dress and a smile and walked in alone. Except she didn't remain alone. Blake, oddly enough, had spent the majority of the time at her side, attentive in a way that was almost protective. He'd even made a point of getting her alone for a few minutes to ask for her version of her and Tate's broken engagement and how she was handling it, then made his offer to take her home early.

He briefly glanced her way. "No apologies necessary. Seeing Tate with someone else can't have been easy."

"No, but not in the way you mean," she told him honestly. "It's more my having to make explanations to everyone as to why we broke things off."

"He hurt you—"

"I told you before, at the party, it's not like that." Katie sighed, not sure how to explain her feelings any more clearly than she'd tried earlier. Blake wasn't a man who inspired confidences. Unlike Tate, whom she could easily read, she was never quite sure what Blake was thinking, what emotions lay behind the cool, aloof face he presented to the world. That he was Tate's brother—longtime friend or not—made this whole conversation, their being together at all, strange and more than a little uncomfortable.

She repeated the assertion she'd made to him the first time. "A marriage between Tate and me wouldn't have worked. We've both known it for a while now. I care about Tate, I always will. But there wasn't any… passion between us."

"You were lovers."

Katie felt herself flush, glad for the covering darkness. "It's not the same thing. Neither of us ever felt compelled to be together. There was never anything overwhelming about what we felt for each other."

"That sounds like Tate talking," Blake said tightly.

"You seem determined to blame him. But believe me, it was a mutual decision. I'm just feeling a little… lost, I guess. Tate and I were together for so long. It's the starting over part of this that isn't easy."

She didn't expect Blake to understand. In all the time she'd known him, the women he'd dated seemed nothing more than accessories to him, the obligatory beautiful and well-dressed companions for the social events he attended and, she assumed, casual lovers. Against her long-term attachment to Tate—cultivated by their families from childhood—Blake would have no basis for comparison.

"It may have been mutual, but as far as I'm concerned, he treated you badly. He never appreciated what he had in you. All those years you were together, I wouldn't have called him faithful or even considerate a good part of the time. You didn't deserve that."

The underlying anger in his tone surprised her. She wouldn't have pictured Blake in the role of her defender and yet she had the impression this wasn't the first time he'd voiced these opinions, probably to Tate. It left her more confused about who he was and what she wanted.

The conversation lagged the remainder of the ride and the short walk from his car to the front door of the Salgar estate Katie still called home. Awkwardness took hold, at least on her part, as she hunted for the conventional courteous phrases to release him from any further obligation to her and finally end what had been several taxing hours.

"Thank you for bringing me home," she said. "It was nice of you to take the trouble."

He was looking at her with an odd expression she couldn't decipher. "It was hardly the chore you're making it out to be."

"I appreciate it all the same." She hesitated before adding, "Good night, Blake."

She expected an echoing rejoinder and him leaving. Instead he let several moments pass before reaching out and tracing his fingertips over her cheek.

His touch, gentle and unexpected, hitched her breath. "Blake…"

Under any circumstances, she wouldn't have anticipated him touching her like this, let alone taking it further. But when he did, she couldn't think of a reason he shouldn't. She couldn't *think* at all.

He moved closer and, drawn by the intensity of his gaze, she matched him until they stood lightly pressed against each other. Bending to her, he brushed her lips with his, the barest touch at first. It teased her senses, giving her a taste of the wine he'd drunk, a hint of his heat, the spicy scent of his cologne. She returned the caress in kind, testing the novel sensation of his mouth on hers and finding the scant feeling more enticing than an intimate kiss.

After long seconds, Blake broke the tentative contact to look at her, as though gauging her and his responses. Whatever he saw apparently made up his mind and he slid his hand around her nape, threading his fingers into her hair, bringing her closer at the same time he slanted his mouth over hers.

If he had been aggressively passionate, she would have found him easy to resist. But his kiss, slow and sensual, with a depth of tenderness she never would have guessed he possessed, had her melting into his arms, yielding to a rush of desire so intense that what she'd felt when Tate held her suddenly seemed pale in contrast.

It was impossible. This was *Blake*. They couldn't— and it didn't matter because she was kissing him back, her hands on his shoulders, his free hand splayed low on her back molding her body to his, and her world in that brief time narrowed to him.

She might have given into temporary madness and allowed her feelings to seduce her into inviting more intimacy than a few kisses, but Blake didn't give her the chance. Almost abruptly, he stepped back from their embrace and from his slightly stunned look she knew he'd been as caught off guard as she by the feelings he'd exposed.

He half raised a hand as if to touch her again then let it drop. "Good night, Katie," he said softly.

He left her in the pool of light on her doorstep, watching him stride away and fighting the urge to call him back....

"Katie?"

Slim fingers waved in front of her face, jolting Katie back to the present.

Her assistant, Tessa Lansing, stood at her side, with a handful of papers and the twitch of her lips threatening to become a grin. "I've got the information on those grant proposals you wanted but it looks like you're somewhere else a lot more interesting than here. Whoever he is, he must be somebody special."

"I was just thinking," Katie said quickly, sure her face was as red as Tessa's bobbed curls.

"I got that. But that look on your face begs the question about *whom?*"

Coming from anyone else, the blunt curiosity about her personal life would have been irritating. Tessa, though, was a friend and after eight years of working closely together, helping Katie in her position as administrator of the Salgar's charitable foundation, there wasn't much about Katie's moods that escaped Tessa's notice.

"No one in particular," she said lightly.

Tessa eyed her over the top of her glasses. "Right. I've never seen you look like that even when you talked about Tate. Sorry," she added at Katie's small frown, "I'm sure that's a sore subject right now."

"I am getting tired of everyone assuming Tate dumped me for Tanya Kimbrough or that I left him because he treated me badly and that either way, I'm devastated."

"Oh, I see," Tessa teased. "You're saying you dumped him for the guy that makes you all dreamy-eyed."

"No, and I wasn't all dreamy-eyed. Let me take a look at those," Katie said, taking the papers from Tessa to change the subject.

But the subject—Blake McCord—was no more easily dismissed in her thoughts than he was in person.

Nearly a week had passed since that kiss that shouldn't have happened and she should have forgotten. Except she couldn't forget, and forbidden or not, she couldn't rid herself of the restless, indefinable longings he'd stirred up in her.

If things were different, she would have avoided him until she could sort out the tangled mess that was her feelings these days. But she and Blake were the primary planners for the Dallas Children's Hospital's major annual fund-raising ball, and at this phase of the preparations, she couldn't limit their contact to phone calls and e-mails without compromising efficiency.

In fact…she glanced at her watch. In a few hours, because of the scheduled hospital board meeting, they would be in close company again. She didn't know what to expect, from him or herself. Would he pretend it never happened and nothing had changed between them? Or—and this was the more daunting option—would he want to confront it, either dismissing it as a moment's impulse or acknowledging it was something more?

Uncertain how to answer herself, Katie was less sure which alternative made her more uneasy.

Blake McCord stared at the electronic display of times and dates telling him where he was supposed to be today, not really seeing the neatly plotted schedule, but instead having an all-too-real vision of disaster.

He was fast running out of time. Unless he could pull

off the risky scheme he'd devised to rescue McCord Jewelers, there might be little left to salvage from the wreckage of the family fortunes. There was no question about his determination to succeed. But he didn't like the odds that the entire plot would blow up in his face and leave him with an even worse situation.

Wishing for other options was a waste of time. He'd committed himself to carrying this through, despite the dangers. There was no going back.

"This is becoming a bad habit with you." Seated at the head of the table, Eleanor McCord frowned at the brief glance her oldest son gave her in acknowledgment. "I don't know why you bother coming to meals anymore. It's obvious that business has all your attention."

"I'm sorry," Blake said shortly. He put aside his BlackBerry long enough to finish off the last of his coffee, wondering at the same time why he did bother. This morning, in particular, he should have avoided a breakfast tête-à-tête with his mother in favor of the relative solitude of his office. He had enough on his mind these days without adding family issues to the mix. "I'm juggling a number of things and they're all priority at the moment."

Eleanor didn't respond at once but instead studied him. "You never share your responsibilities," she observed after a moment. "I can't remember a time when you allowed yourself to share the load."

"That would be because they are *my* responsibilities. Besides, It's not like anyone has exactly begged me for the opportunity."

"Perhaps, but nonetheless, I'm concerned about the effect that whatever this latest crisis is having on you. I don't think I've ever seen you quite as irritable and distant as you've been these past few weeks. I'm assuming the situation with the business is worse off than you've been saying. Or is it something else?"

"It's nothing you need to worry about." The lie came out smoothly.

"It's not that, so much," Eleanor said. "I'm worried about you."

"That would be a first," he retorted, immediately regretting it.

Under other circumstances, he would never have let his feelings slip. But things between him and his mother had been more tense than usual since Eleanor had revealed that an affair twenty-two years ago between her and Rex Foley, patriarch of the rival Foley clan, had produced Blake's youngest brother Charlie. That her late husband, Devon McCord, had apparently never known Charlie wasn't his son hadn't made Eleanor's confession any easier for her four other children to accept. What with the weight of being solely liable for the family business's survival or collapse coupled with the knowledge of his mother's betrayal, Blake silently admitted his temper was more than a little frayed. It was straining all his relationships, but particularly those with his family. He and Eleanor had never shared a warm, close bond, but her admission had severely tested the link there was.

Still, he hated his inability to keep his emotions in check. Shoving them aside, he made an effort to backtrack. "Everything is fine, or will be soon. I just need a few more weeks to straighten things out."

Eleanor's raised brow telegraphed her annoyance. "I'm not stupid, Blake. I know there are problems. Your father's spending habits were hardly a secret. Sometimes I still find it hard to believe how much money he managed to go through in a relatively short time. I know he didn't do the business any good, and with the retail market the way it is, McCord's must be suffering."

"If there are problems, I'll take care of them," Blake said, getting to his feet, deliberately ignoring the familiar criticism of his father. He, better than anyone, knew how many millions Devon had squandered on maintaining the lavish lifestyle he thought he was entitled to. "I always do."

"Blake—"

"I have to go. I have a full schedule and a board meeting at the hospital this morning," he explained referring to his seat on the board at Dallas Children's Hospital.

"Will Katie be there?" Eleanor asked.

At the mention of his brother's former fiancée, Blake retreated further behind carefully constructed indifference. "I would assume so. She is a board member."

"You're working together planning the Halloween ball, aren't you?" At Blake's curt nod, Eleanor appraised him in silence for a moment, then gave a small sigh. "It's a shame she and Tate couldn't have worked things out, they were so well suited. Although he and Tanya seem very happy together, so I suppose it's all for the best. I wonder about Katie, though, if she's been accepting of their breakup and Tate becoming engaged again so quickly as Tate claims."

Blake sensed his mother still harbored reservations about Tate's romance with Tanya Kimbrough. Scant weeks had passed between Tate breaking his engagement to Katie and deciding Tanya, the McCord's housekeeper's daughter, was the love of his life. Blake had doubts, too, but he kept them to himself, not wanting to encourage any hopes his mother might have that Tate and Katie would reconcile.

"Katie appears to be handling it well," Blake said dismissively.

On the road to his office a few minutes later, he wished his mother hadn't mentioned Katie. With everything demanding his attention, he didn't need another distraction and yet he found himself too often thinking about the one woman who never should have entered his mind—his brother's ex.

For months now, and especially since the night of the Labor Day party, he'd caught himself watching her, finding reasons to talk to her, thinking about her even before she and Tate split up and when his focus should have wholly been on business.

And that night… The memory still had the power to eclipse all others despite his best attempts to exorcise it and reject it as nothing more than a fleeting impulse on his part.

He had told himself his offer to take her home was a friend's gesture, to help ease her awkwardness at being the center of speculation at the party, the hurt she denied but he had to believe she felt seeing Tate in love with another woman. He could make a case for that up until the moment he touched her. Then he'd kissed her, his fingers tangled in her dark, thick hair, her soft curves pressed against him, and he knew he shouldn't have, but damn it, it had felt too good, too right to stop.

Before, as Tate's girlfriend, then fiancée, she'd been off-limits. He still wasn't allowed to want her, though she was no longer his brother's woman. She was vulnerable after her breakup with Tate and he had no business exploiting it to satisfy his own desires. Katie needed someone who would cherish her, commit to a loving, lasting relationship. In that respect, he was definitely not the man for her, or anyone else.

Despite that, he couldn't seem to control his feelings when it came to her and his lack of control irritated him. It also made him more determined to act the strict professional today at the board meeting. Most likely, she'd decided the same thing. They could ignore what had happened and go back to being friends working together to accomplish a common goal.

He convinced himself of it as he strode into the boardroom, ready for business.

Except, following him inside was an invisible companion that taunted him for his prick of disappointment when he didn't see her among the group, an inner voice that called him a liar and questioned whether forgetting was going to be as easy as he expected.

Chapter Two

Where was she? Blake tugged the white cuff of his shirtsleeve back and for the third time in ten minutes glanced at his watch. Would Katie actually skip the board meeting to avoid seeing him?

It was only a kiss.

If that were true, then why did his insides still turn at the memory of her willing lips? Why did his fingers ache for the feel of her hair twined between them, his senses yearn for the scent of her musky perfume?

"I'm sorry to keep everyone waiting."

The rich melody of her voice brought his eyes up, meeting hers. She stood across from him at the massive boardroom table; their eyes caught and held moments too long. A fact he knew didn't go unnoticed by the other board members.

Katie broke their gaze, glanced quickly around the

room. "I had a last-minute delay," she said, smoothing her black pencil skirt to her slim thighs before taking her seat opposite Blake.

She looked perfect, as usual, he noted, the teal of her silk blouse accenting her dark eyes and hair, the sensual curve of her mouth as she spoke drawing the attention of every male in the room, an observation that made Blake both jealous and proud—though he realized one touch to those lips gave him no right to be.

At the head of the table, the board president called the meeting to order and laid out the agenda. Blake heard him drone on, but only from a distance. He couldn't manage to focus on anything but the woman sitting in silence, quietly stealing his attention, too far away to touch, close enough to capture his every thought.

"Blake, you *will* take care of those paintings for the silent auction, won't you? Blake—are you with us?"

Katie's eyes fixed on him. "Blake," she whispered across the table. "Evan is talking to you."

"Of course I will." Blake turned sharply toward the man at the head of the table and said tersely, "I told you I would a month ago, didn't I?" He hoped his tone would be a save for his embarrassingly distracted state.

"Good. *Sorry,* I didn't think you were listening," Evan Rutherford returned, matching Blake's insolence.

Blake faced Katie. "You and your family know the Kenningtons better than I do. They might be more generous with their donations if you joined me when I go talk to them."

Katie's lashes fluttered once as she blinked back a look of awkward surprise that amused Blake. "I—of course, I'll be happy to visit them with you. I'm quite familiar with their collection."

"Thank you." He'd put her on the spot publicly and after the barest hint of a falter, she'd responded with her usual grace. But the look she gave him now said he'd be hearing about this later.

"Very well," Evan pronounced with typical condescension. "I trust you two will manage to secure a few excellent pieces for the auction. Now moving on to the remainder of the donations…"

Again Blake tuned Evan out. With a flip of his Black-Berry, he could call in favors across the country to bring in a number of high-ticket items for the auction, in addition to the Kenningtons' artworks and he hardly needed Rutherford to tell him how to do it.

What he did need was time alone with Katie. Seeing her again after spending too much time wondering what she'd been thinking, feeling since that night they'd kissed intensified his need to know. Damn this meeting, anyway. It was taking forever. They'd all done these charity events dozens of times before. Why were they wasting his time on details he knew by rote memory, wasting hours he could be using much more productively? He had to get back to the office soon. Deciding to take control of the situation, he motioned to Evan.

"Are we about done here? I have another meeting."

Rutherford cleared his throat loudly. "Well—er…"

"Good." Blake shoved his chair back and turned from the older man to Katie. "May I have a word with you before I leave?"

Again, Katie shielded her thoughts from the rest of the room, allowing for his eyes only a flash of agitation. "Certainly. Will you all excuse me for a moment please? Obviously, Blake is on a tight schedule. As usual."

He followed her out into the hallway of the administrative wing of the hospital. The second he closed the door behind them, she planted the palms of her perfectly manicured hands on the curves of her hips and fixed him with a frown.

"If you weren't a McCord, Evan would have kicked you off the board by now, you know that? He doesn't take well to interruptions or usurpations of his authority. Yet you manage to pull them off at nearly every board meeting."

"Evan can go straight to hell."

"Well, you're certainly in a mood today."

"So I've been told. Is there some reason you've been avoiding me?"

She glanced away, letting her palms slide from her hips down the front of her skirt. "I haven't been avoiding you."

"It's interesting, then, that I haven't heard a word from you since the Labor Day party. We are supposed to be working together on this fund-raiser."

"That doesn't mean we need to be in constant contact, does it?"

"Are you angry about that night?" Blake asked her bluntly. "Angry I kissed you?"

Her eyes brightened, her lips parting for a too-light and casual laugh that sounded forced. "What, that? Oh, Blake, really. I'm not a schoolgirl. It was a simple kiss good-night. Nothing more. We both know that."

His eyes narrowed on her. "You're lying."

"Don't flatter yourself."

"I don't have to. I've known you since you *were* a schoolgirl, remember?"

Her bravado left her then. "Touché." She paused and took a deep breath. "No, I'm not angry," she said softly. "It was…I don't know—nice."

"Nice?" She nodded and he scowled. "I don't think I've ever been told that before."

"Well, I'm sorry if that doesn't flatter your ego, but somehow I think it will survive intact without my stroking it."

Blake found himself taking a step closer. "You think so?"

"I doubt my opinion of you matters," she said levelly, but he noticed the quickened pace of her breath, the slight flush in her face.

"It matters." Gently, he traced his knuckles down her cheek. "It matters a lot."

She looked back at him, her dark eyes pooling with a mixture of emotions, drawing him to plunge in.

Then the schedule alarm on his BlackBerry beeped, breaking the mood. Blake swore under his breath.

"You'd better go or you'll miss your meeting," Katie said.

"I'll call you later today about meeting with the Kenningtons."

"No rush," she returned lightly, renewing the tension Blake had been battling for the last week.

"Just keep your phone on." Irritated and feeling she'd somehow taken control and gotten the best of him, he turned on his heel, determined to ensure the next round with Miss Cool and Collected Whitcomb-Salgar would be his.

When the last trace of his broad shoulders disappeared around the hallway corner, Katie released the breath she'd been holding and leaned against the wall. Had she succeeded in hiding the past week's daydreams, memories, questions, guilt and desire his single kiss evoked in her? Judging from his reaction, she'd have to guess she had. So why didn't it feel more satisfying to know she'd fooled him into thinking that night—that kiss—didn't matter?

She glanced at her watch. She should get back to her office, too, but she'd told the other board members she'd rejoin the meeting. Desperately wanting to escape, she reluctantly went back into the boardroom to face a dozen sets of curious eyes.

The rest of the meeting passed in a blur, her thoughts unresolved, miles away in a different moment and place.

As if the day hadn't been long and difficult enough, Blake's arrival home only added pressure on pressure.

"So I heard you walked out on the board meeting at the hospital today and pissed everyone off, particularly Evan," Tate said as he met Blake in the library of the McCord mansion, drink in hand. "Everyone but Katie, that is."

Blake poured himself a scotch on the rocks. "If our company worked as efficiently as the gossip mill around here did, we'd be thriving instead of drowning."

Tate's brows drew close. "So no progress yet."

"All I can say is the PR campaign had better work miracles, and Paige had better get busy finding the Santa Magdalena Diamond, or we're sunk."

He was relying on his younger sister, the geologist and gemologist, to locate the famous canary diamond as part of his efforts to restore the McCord fortunes. The diamond was supposed to be hidden in an abandoned mine on Travis Foley's ranch, which made the task of retrieving it all the more difficult. Though the McCord family held the deed to the ranch, if the Foleys got wind of what they were up to, Blake was certain they'd find a way to sabotage his plans. He hated having to depend on Paige, but this was one element of his master plan he couldn't pull off himself.

He downed the shot of scotch. It burned slightly as it slid down his throat, but the pain was a welcome distraction from the pain in his head. "Speaking of that, is Paige around?"

"I haven't seen her yet this evening." Tate paused, swirling the ice in his glass. "So what's this I hear about you and Katie whispering in the hospital hallway?"

Blake jerked back a little. "What's it to you who Katie's whispering to? You broke things off with her."

"I did not and you know it. It was mutual—and it was her idea first. Katie's free to whisper to anyone she cares to. But it just looks strange for my brother to be disrupting a meeting to pull my ex out into the hall for a little tête-à-tête."

"That's ridiculous," he said, knowing it was a lie. "Who's been talking to you?" Though he'd rather walk on hot coals than admit he had any interest in Katie, internally he tensed. The truth was he couldn't get her off his mind and a part of him felt oddly guilty because of it.

When he'd seen her today, his first thought was to taste those tempting lips again. His second was to get her alone and taste a lot more than that. That's where he'd stopped himself from mentally drifting any further into fantasies about his brother's former fiancée.

"To me?" Tate was saying. "No one. But Evan called Mom after the meeting and apparently he was pretty put off about the whole thing."

"Evan needs to get a life. And so does everyone else who's trying to make something out of nothing. I had to leave and before I did I needed to make plans with Katie to help me wring a few pricey paintings out of the Kenningtons. End of story. Not that it's any of your business."

"What's none of his business?" Paige asked, waltzing into the room. Blond and beautiful as her mother and her twin, Penny, Paige's eyes sparked mischief as she perched on the edge of an armchair.

"Don't you start, too. Isn't any damned thing private around here?" Blake muttered, refilling his glass.

"Are you kidding?"

"Right. What was I thinking?"

"So, what's the big secret Tate isn't supposed to know?" she asked.

Blake skipped answering her question. "I needed to talk to you. I've got some new information on the mine. It's not much but I thought I'd pass it on in case it helped."

"Really?" Paige asked, looking interested. "What?"

"It has to do with the interior configuration and passages. I have the specifics at my office. Drop by tomorrow and I'll show them to you."

"Sure. I have to run now, though. I want to catch a lecture on a rare Chinese black pearl at the museum of gemology."

"Sounds thrilling," Tate teased.

"Beats the heck out of scrubs, blood and needles," she quipped in reference to Tate's position as a surgeon at Meridien General Hospital.

"Okay, okay, point taken."

Paige waved a hand goodbye and left the room, humming some new tune Blake had heard on the radio but couldn't name. He was counting on his little sister to come through for him and secure the Santa Magdalena Diamond or—or *nothing*. He didn't want to think about the *or* because at this point there wasn't one.

Tate finished his drink and flipped open his cell, punching in a number, smiling when the person at the other end picked up. "Hey, babe, you ready? I'm done here." He paused, listening, then with a "Love you, too," punched the off button.

"How's Tanya?" Blake asked since it was obvious Tate had been making plans with his new love. Though he couldn't resist giving Tate some grief over his treatment of Katie, actually Blake was happy his brother seemed to have found a true soul mate in Tanya.

"Great. Perfect. We're meeting some friends for dinner at that new bistro downtown so I need to get going."

"Give her my best," Blake offered, glad to see his brother relaxed and enjoying his new relationship, despite the pain and awkwardness the whole breakup with Katie had created.

That was in the past and Tate now seemed genuinely satisfied. Katie, on the other hand, seemed conflicted. Suddenly he remembered he'd told her he'd call before the day's end. He checked his watch. Eight o'clock already. Too late to call? Probably, but somehow he didn't care. He wanted to see her as an antidote to the day's tensions, though, through no fault of her own, she'd been a contributing cause.

"Sorry it's so late," he said when he heard her soft voice at the other end of the line.

"I thought you'd forgotten."

"No, just a long day. How about a nightcap?" He threw out the invitation casually, then waited, hoping the long pause wasn't a signal he was wasting his time.

At the other end of the line Katie considered his offer. All afternoon she'd been haunted by confused feelings, conflicting emotions of guilt over the chance that she might be attracted to Tate's brother and excitement over the possibility that Blake might be attracted to her.

Against her better judgment, she finally answered, "Sure. Sounds *nice*," she teased recalling to him her description of his kiss—which was so much more than *nice* she scarcely dared admit it to herself.

"I have to do something about this *nice* stuff. It's going to ruin my image."

She laughed a little and they arranged to meet at an intimate club situated in town about halfway between the McCord and Salgar estates.

Katie rushed to change into a little designer cocktail dress and strappy heels and to freshen her makeup. Lining her lips in a shimmering pink tone that flattered her skin, eyes and hair, she gazed at herself in the mirror, realizing she'd never before felt compelled to primp for Blake. He was just a friend after all. Now, though…uncertainty washed over her as she imagined a ghost of Tate at her side in the mirror.

"This is ridiculous," she muttered, stuffing the lipstick into her beaded evening bag, reminding herself she and Tate had agreed to move on with their lives and without each other.

Twenty minutes later, after the valet had taken the keys to her Jaguar, she entered the dark club, her eyes adjusting to dim lighting and low tables with black tablecloths and silver candles.

She felt a large, warm hand on her lower back. "You look beautiful." Blake's appreciative remark sent a shiver down her spine only to disappear beneath his touch.

"Oh, you startled me. I didn't see you there."

"I have a table for us." He pointed to an intimate booth in a corner near the elegant marble-topped bar.

"Looks like you had a few to choose from. Small crowd tonight."

"Midweek." He shrugged, motioning her to lead the way.

As she sat down, she saw that he'd already ordered her favorite white Bordeaux. Lifting the glass appreciatively, she smiled. "You've known me too long."

He slid in beside her and as her eyes adjusted she noticed he too had changed from his business suit to a more casual black turtleneck and blazer, a look she definitely appreciated.

"On the contrary, lately I've begun to feel like I'm just beginning to know you."

Her nerves jumpy, Katie took a sip of wine to calm them. "Is that so?"

"Very much. In fact, I'm looking forward to working with you more closely on the Halloween ball. I have the feeling I'm going to see sides of you I've never seen before."

"You make me sound more complex than I am. I'm the same old Katie you've always known."

"There's nothing the same or old about you. It's not really fair, you know," he mused, resting back in his seat, "wearing a dress like that when we're supposed to discuss business. Looking at you, how am I supposed to think straight?"

"Since when do you waste compliments on me? Save them for those supermodels you seem to like to decorate your arm with."

"They're wasted on them," he said in a low voice she almost took for serious.

He couldn't be, though she didn't understand this change in him. He'd always been coolly polite to her, solicitous even, but never flirtatious or suggestive, nor had he ever given her the slightest indication he considered her anything else but his brother's fiancée. This shift in his attentions to her was unsettling because she didn't know how to respond.

Deciding to take control of the conversation, she brought up plans for donations for the ball. Obligatorily, he answered her questions, agreed to her ideas, added a few of his own.

"As a team, I've no doubt we'll bring in more top-dollar auction items than the rest of them put together," he said.

"Ever the indefatigable confidence. I'm glad you have it because I'm concerned this year. People aren't as generous in times like this."

He leaned a little closer. "Katie?"

Wondering at the intensity of his tone, she met his gaze. "Yes?"

"Can we change the subject?"

"I—of course. But I thought that's why you asked me here."

"It wasn't."

Her stomach fluttered and she wasn't sure if she wanted to ask the obvious question. She did it anyhow. "Then why?"

"It was a demanding day for a lot of reasons and the one way I realized I could actually relax and enjoy the evening was to spend it with you."

Now he wasn't teasing. She knew him that well. His honesty touched her, reflected her own feelings about seeing him again tonight. "I'm glad," she said quietly, "because I wanted to see you again, too."

"I'd like to do more of that."

Wanting the same, nonetheless she lowered her eyes. Where was this going? It should stop here, before it really started. She'd ended her engagement only weeks ago; she had no business throwing herself into another relationship so soon, especially a relationship with Tate's brother.

"Isn't there another fund-raiser for your uncle coming up in a week or so?" Blake interrupted her inner debate.

Katie nodded, though his question, seemingly off topic, caught her off guard. Her uncle, Peter Salgar, was making a bid for governor, and the upcoming gala was one of many she'd attended over the last year in support of his campaign. "I can't say I'm looking forward to it, but it's difficult to say no."

"I know you usually end up going to those alone."

"If you mean Tate never went with me, you're right. It would have been rather awkward, don't you think?" That was putting it mildly. Scandalous might be a better description. One of her uncle's strongest supporters was Rex Foley and the McCords had traditionally backed Peter's opponent in this race, Adam Trent.

"Why don't you let me escort you?" Blake offered.

"You?" Katie shook her head. "I couldn't ask you to do that. Your family would disown you."

"You aren't asking, I'm volunteering. And as for my family, whom I spend my time with and where is my business."

"I don't think your mother will see it that way."

"I'm well beyond the age of needing my mother's permission, or her approval." Reaching across the table, he touched her hand. "Say yes."

If it were merely a simple party, the answer would have tripped off her lips easily. She enjoyed every moment they'd spent together at such events as friends. But now, given her breakup with Tate, the fact that most of the Foleys would be at the fund-raiser, and there would be many people there taking critical note of her escort, in addition to the lingering memory of how much she'd enjoyed their one kiss, she felt confused, hesitant.

"I want to go with you and I appreciate the offer but—"

"I understand," he said gently, and she feared he truly did. "I'll have your car brought around."

He seemed disappointed, though his brief half smile exhibited a sincere attempt to hide his feelings.

Without thinking of the consequences, she blurted out, "I'd love to. To go with you," she amended at his confused look. "Thank you. It was nice of you to suggest it."

His expression relaxed and he gave an appreciative nod. "There's that word again. I promise, my intentions are purely to ward off all those people who want to ask questions about you and Tate."

"Thanks, but I can take care of myself. I'll just enjoy not having to show up alone." That much was true. She delighted at the idea of walking into the fund-raiser on Blake's arm. Unfortunately, her mind wouldn't let her enjoy that notion freely, though. It came with weighted strings attached.

"Will you let me bring your car around now?"

"Oh, no need. I valeted." She took her ticket out of her purse and with a slight brush of her lips to his cheek, eased away from him. "Please, stay and finish your drink. Thank you again for the wine."

For a moment she thought he might get up and follow her out, but after moving in that direction, he seemed to think better of it and stayed put. "Send me a text when you get home, okay? Let me know you got there safely."

Turning from him, her mind and emotions locked in internal warfare, she managed a smile and a lighthearted "Will do" before slipping out into the night.

Chapter Three

A dozen important things demanded her attention and there were other places she ought to be, but Katie, desperately needing a distraction or a confidant—she wasn't sure which—had temporarily put them aside for a long lunch with a friend. She hadn't planned on the outing today—on top of everything else, she was hosting a dinner tonight for several potential donors to the children's hospital benefit—but when Gabriella called, Katie had jumped at Gabby's invitation.

Gabby, Blake's beautiful blond cousin, had recently wed Rafael Balthazer, the head of security for McCord Jewelers, and the couple had decided to make their home in Italy. But at Blake's request, Gabby was back in Dallas for a short stay, doing some modeling for McCord's as part of the PR campaign Blake had recently launched.

"Marriage obviously agrees with you," Katie said, after the waiter had left with their orders. "I know it's a cliché, but you're positively glowing."

"Being in love will do that." Setting down her wine-glass, Gabby fixed her with a slight frown. "You, on the other hand, are not glowing. Just the opposite in fact. What's wrong? Is it the breakup with Tate?"

"Not really," Katie hedged. "That's been difficult but not nearly as awful as everyone seems to believe." At Gabby' expectant look, she gave in. "It's Blake."

"Ah. I was wondering how long it would take him."

"How long it would take him to do what?"

"Whatever it is that he's done to upset you."

The waiter interrupted, bringing their salads, and Katie waited until he'd left before saying firmly, "He hasn't upset me. But I didn't expect—" She broke off, not sure if she meant to confess about him kissing her, his new attentiveness or her confused feelings.

"I've suspected for a while from things he's said and the way he looks at you that there was something between you two, at least on his part. I'm not the only one who's noticed, either. If it hadn't been for Tate I think Blake would have done something about it a long time ago." Gabby shrugged off Katie's skepticism. "Don't take this the wrong way, but I hope you know what you're doing getting involved with someone so soon after Tate, especially a man like Blake."

"I'm not *involved* with him, but even if I were, what's so terrible about Blake that you feel the need to warn me away?"

"I didn't say terrible," Gabby said carefully. "But Blake is—difficult. He's not exactly a warm, open person. As far as I know, he's never had a serious relationship, which is not surprising considering how demanding he is. I'm not sure you're ready for the challenge."

"Just because he's focused and takes his responsibilities seriously, doesn't make him difficult," Katie responded, with more force than she intended. "And I know I can rely on him. I cared for Tate, I still do, but he was never the devoted type, at least with me," she said, echoing Blake's criticism of his brother. "If I hadn't been raised to believe we'd end up together one day, I doubt I would have stayed with him as long as I did."

Gabby started on her salad. "If I were you, I'd rethink that denial about not being involved with Blake."

"It's the truth. We're friends, nothing else." Inwardly, she winced, aware of the waver in her voice that betrayed her uncertainty. Yet she doubted that Blake had been as affected by their brief encounters, and she was wary of admitting anything she felt was more complicated than a weak moment on her part. He'd made it clear he found her attractive and had, in typical fashion, taken charge and acted on it. She was vulnerable, finding her way in the wake of her broken engagement, and had surrendered to temptation. Why did it have to be anything other than that?

"Whether it's true or not, if people keep seeing you together, they're going to talk about your preference for McCord men," Gabby cautioned her.

Not wanting to admit it to Gabby, Katie found the idea she could be seriously attracted to Blake a little embarrassing. Her friend was right, people would talk, and the gossip wouldn't flatter either her or Blake. She could only imagine his reaction to that. Thinking about it, she was seriously starting to regret accepting his offer to escort her to her uncle's fund-raiser. It was only going to convince some people, like Gabby, that there was more between them than friendship and a temporary working partnership.

"I can't stop people from talking, but I'm not certain what my preferences are right now." Yet even as she said it, she saw Blake. "I've never given any thought to what I want in a relationship and until I do, I don't intend to get too deeply involved with Blake or anyone else. It wouldn't be fair to either of us." She smiled at Gabby, hoping she radiated confidence. It was a sensible speech, a reasonable plan for the future.

But inwardly, Katie thought sense and reason didn't have much to do with desires and it was going to be difficult to stick to her guns when it came to Blake McCord.

Her determination to try, though, carried her through the rest of the day and into the evening, allowing her to maintain a veneer of aloofness when she greeted him in the elegantly appointed living room an hour before the guests were due to arrive.

There were questions in his eyes at her shift in attitude, but he didn't comment and, taking his cue from her, his manner toward her was a shade cooler.

"I haven't had the chance to tell you, but I had a call from the caterer this afternoon. They apparently had a scheduling problem and they've cancelled," she said, handing him a glass of wine. His fingers brushed hers and lingered for brief seconds, as did his gaze on the smooth skin and hint of cleavage exposed by her sleeveless dress. Her breath quickened and she turned slightly aside. "I've found a replacement, a firm your mother recommended. I tried to call you before I booked them, but you weren't answering your cell."

Blake's mouth quirked at the corner in a sardonic half smile. "You don't need my permission to make decisions, Katie."

"I know you're accustomed to taking the lead," she answered with a small smile of her own. "I'm pretty certain teamwork isn't one of your favorite strategies."

"Guilty as charged. But you're quite capable of taking the lead yourself. I'm impressed you were able to find a replacement so quickly. I doubt I could have handled the situation any better."

"It was hardly a crisis. But thank you, that *is* a compliment."

"You sound surprised." Blake moved by her a few steps with the apparent intent of studying one of the large landscapes on the wall, stopping within a hand's distance of her. His focus on the painting, he added, "I do give them occasionally."

"From what I know, very occasionally," she said, softening her tone to a gentle teasing, though she herself had more than once thought him cold and critical of others' opinions or actions, especially when it came to his business. Yet over the years, she'd come to realize that he was most critical of himself, demanding perfection of himself and expecting no less in others. She had never really given it much consideration, accepting it as part of him, but she wondered now what drove him to put so much pressure on himself. It could be arrogance, him believing no one else could do it better than he. Some instinct balked at accepting that simple explanation, though. There was nothing that simple about Blake.

Abandoning his appraisal of the painting, he faced her. "You don't seem to have a very high opinion of me," he said dryly. "I'm guessing that's the reason why we've gone back to being polite acquaintances."

"That's not it at all." Her eyes slewed from his steady gaze to his hands, one clasped around his glass. It was ridiculous to crave a touch, so strongly desire the warmth of a caress; to feel those needs all the more intensely from simply a glance his direction. How could she, who couldn't claim to have ever been swept away by passion, want so much?

"If it's easier for you to pretend that nothing happened—"

Katie raised her eyes, saw an inscrutable expression in the steel-gray of his. "No, I don't want to pretend. But it's…complicated."

"I suppose it is, if we make it that way."

"It can't be any other way, for me." And it troubled her he apparently didn't understand or share her conflicted emotions.

He replied with silence, watching her in a way that made her feel he was weighing her words, judging her honesty. "Then it's complicated," he said finally. "But it doesn't have to be impossible."

"I need to decide that for myself. I've let everybody tell me what's right for me for too long now. It's time I make my own choices."

She half expected he'd take offense, but to her surprise Blake smiled. "Fair enough. But I hope, at least once in a while, you'll give me the opportunity to influence those choices."

Not waiting for her answer, he took a step closer and lightly kissed her, touching her only with his mouth. The lingering caress flushed her with a slow, curling heat and briefly erased every reason she'd given herself that this was a bad idea. If the door chime, announcing the first of her guests, hadn't intruded, she suspected Blake might have convinced her to forget reason completely and act on her desires.

She thought Blake knew that from the almost smug satisfaction in his face and the way he stayed next to her to greet the new arrivals as if they were a couple, hosting the evening together. She liked the feeling he always seemed to be there when she most appreciated having someone at her side; she was unnerved by how much she liked it. More unnerving was how much she liked him touching her.

This shouldn't happen between them, not so soon after her broken engagement, maybe not ever. And yet, putting on the face of hostess, she couldn't shake the sensation that somehow, some way, it had become inevitable.

Never a fan of these sorts of gatherings, Blake found new reasons for his distaste the longer the evening progressed. Most of the guests, the women in particular, preferred hearing about Katie's personal life over her appeal for the hospital. He knew it wasn't the first time she'd had to put up with the whisperings behind her back and the less than subtle probing to her face, but tonight he found it unusually grating.

After dinner, in the middle of making small talk with one of the hospital's bigger benefactors, Blake shifted slightly to bring Katie into his view. She'd been cornered by Selina Harrington and from her stiff posture and the flush in her cheeks, the conversation wasn't going well. Excusing himself, he strode over and slid a hand against her waist, smiling at her when she looked up with a slight start.

"I'm sorry to interrupt, but Parker was asking about the plans for expanding the orthopedic wing. If you wouldn't mind, you're better with those details than I am."

She thanked him with her eyes. "Of course," she said, glancing to Selina. "If you'll excuse me—"

"You two seem very cozy," Selina commented once Katie was gone. Her smile was brittle, a gesture that didn't extend beyond the movement of her carefully painted mouth. "All this togetherness and solicitous concern is so unlike you, Blake."

"Obviously you don't know me as well as you seem to believe," he drawled, the deliberate sardonic cast he put to his words causing her face to tighten. Despite it being three years past, Selina had never forgiven him for turning down her invitation to a casual affair. Selina, former model turned trophy wife, had her attractions but he'd made it clear to her then he never got involved with married women. She, though, had chosen to take his refusal personally.

"Obviously," she snapped. "I thought you had this rule you didn't—how did you so charmingly put it?—take second place when it came to your lovers. Apparently that doesn't include your brother's leftovers." The gibe stung and Selina nodded in satisfaction at his scowl. "So it's true, Katie Whitcomb-Salgar didn't waste any time substituting one McCord man for another. I'd love to know her secrets. Any woman that could convince you to be your brother's replacement must have something special."

He made himself smile, but it was as hard as his voice. "Katie is something special. She's a beautiful, intelligent woman and a friend. But much as I hate to disappoint you and the rest of the gossips who are apparently bored for lack of a scandal, I'm not Tate's replacement and am never going to be."

"Honestly, Blake," Selina said with a harsh laugh, "do you expect anyone to believe that? You spend most of your time looking at her as if you're thinking of everything you want to do to her once you get rid of the rest of us."

Selina's husband coming up to claim his wife saved Blake from a less than honest answer. But rejoining Katie and the conversation of Parker's intended contribution, he couldn't easily discount Selina's observation as pure spite. It made him hyperconscious of his expressions, his gestures around Katie, wondering how much he was betraying without being aware of it.

Even more grating was the idea that he was considered Katie's second choice after Tate. Worse was the unwelcome thought that Katie might look at him that way, as a substitute for the man she loved and desired but couldn't have.

He was still dwelling on it, hours later, when he and Katie said their goodbyes to the last of the guests.

With a sigh, Katie leaned her back to the door. "I always have a hard time enjoying these things. They're too much like work."

"It was quite a success, though. Parker in particular agreed to double his contribution. You should be proud of yourself."

"Yes, that will certainly make a difference," she said slowly. She looked closely at him, frowning slightly. "What's wrong?"

"As you said, these events are too much like work." Aware of the shortness of his tone, he tried to amend it. "It's late and I'm sure you're tired. I should be going."

She ignored his attempt to avoid subjects best left

alone. "Selina said something to you, didn't she, about me taking up with you on the rebound from Tate?"

"She said something along those lines, but it's hardly an issue, is it?"

"Apparently not," she said quietly. Straightening, she turned away from him. "You're right, it's late. Thank you for coming, Blake."

"Katie—"

"I can't stop people from talking." she spun back around. "All I can tell you is they're wrong."

"Are they?"

"Exactly what is that supposed to mean?"

A volatile mix of frustration, banked desire, doubt and anger cracked his facade of indifference and he eliminated the distance between them, grasped her shoulders and covered her mouth with his. He took advantage of her lips, parting in surprise, to kiss her deeply, his tongue sliding along hers in intimate possession. She matched him with a throaty moan that spiked his need and urged him to take what he wanted, what he'd wanted for months, for years but had refused to acknowledge to himself.

He couldn't deny it now. But he hated the idea Katie might be comparing him to Tate; hated more the uneasy feeling that he might not care, that he might be willing to sacrifice his pride if he could have her.

Abruptly, he broke off, breathing hard. "I won't be second-best. Not now, not ever."

Before she could confirm or deny it, he strode past her and out the door, not sure which of them was more shaken by the complete loss of his prized control.

Chapter Four

It was the price they had to pay.

Katie sighed to herself, listening alongside Blake as Pearl Kennington droned on about Katie's broken engagement to Tate and any other tidbit of McCord or Foley gossip she could latch on to. In order to be privy to a showing of possible artworks for donation to the hospital charity ball auction, Blake and Katie were destined to endure luncheon with Pearl. Hal, short for Halbert Kennington, was to join them later.

On her part, she was ready to put up with Pearl for the sake of the children's hospital. It was Blake that worried her. He'd never been easygoing and that he was under pressure was obvious, but she'd never seen him so tense. The way he'd snapped that night at her house had given her a glimpse of the demands he put on himself and hinted at something more unsettling, that he was angry she might compare him to Tate and find him lacking. If he only knew how many times it had been the other way around.

"I simply can't imagine your mama's disappointment, Katie, dear," Pearl was still going on. "I mean after all these years of hopin' and plannin' on your life with Tate. Oh, my, poor Anna. I haven't had the courage to call her. After all, what does one say to a dear, old friend on such a sad occasion?"

"Tate is much happier and so am I," Katie managed, trying to keep the edge out of her voice. "Mother understands that." It was a white lie, but one she had to tell in order to stop the hemorrhaging of gossip and guilt.

"Well, of course that *is* all anyone ever wanted for the both of you," Pearl said with a slight sniff. She raised her delicate teacup, pinky properly uplifted, and glanced absently toward the silver tray of finger cookies.

Blake had sat mostly in silence throughout the ordeal of lunch and dessert. Now, Katie noticed him restlessly drumming his fingers on the arm of his oversize chair. As was the case with every room in the Kenningtons' mansion, furnishings and trappings were overdone. Bigger than life—Texas style—Katie's mother, Anna, had once commented. Anna, who favored elegant understatement in everything from her clothing to the design of her estate, told Katie long ago that the Kenningtons' lifestyle gushed with the same excess as their numerous oil wells did. Nonetheless the two couples had been friends for decades, Anna keeping a polite distance throughout.

A fact that had driven Pearl to near madness. On occasions such as this, she used every moment to go for the social jugular.

"Juanita." She clapped as she called for her maid who stood silently behind them at the ready. "I believe we're finished. Please refresh my guests' coffee so they can take it along on our little tour."

"*Sí*, ma'am." The girl nodded, her eyes bowed.

"I am anxious to view your collection," Blake said, helping Pearl from her chair. "I've heard a lot about the controversial sculpture by that French artist who recently passed away. LeDoux was it?"

"Why yes, such a tragedy. So young. But you know those French…"

Katie scrunched her nose and caught Blake's barely concealed smirk. Standing behind Pearl as she rose, heavy gold bracelets clanking, a serious look swept his expression clear of anything but a studied interest. "Oh, yes, *those* French."

"Precisely," Pearl echoed, satisfied her guests caught her meaning.

Katie fell in beside Blake, who, gallantly, had taken Pearl's arm. They walked, rather nearly crawled, down a seemingly endless corridor, the walls lined with a wealth of paintings to rival a moderately sized city art museum.

Pearl prattled on, shuffling from room to room, describing in tedious detail her proud collection and pointing out a few pieces she might consider donating to the auction. "But, ya'll understand, the final decision is up to Hal."

"Naturally," Blake agreed, continuing to ask politely interested questions while Katie struggled to resist looking at her watch. Then one work in particular caught her eye. She examined it closely, turning to find Blake mesmerized by the same painting.

"This is astounding," she said distractedly.

Blake stepped closer to her and to the painting. They stood in silence several long moments, though within that silence passed a communion of spirit as the painting's effect permeated their hearts and minds.

"It's so simple, yet so profound," Katie said at last.

"I know." Blake's voice had lost it's usual assertiveness, as though humbled by the impact of the artist's rendering of a small child bending to save a lone, wounded duckling from the shore before a rush of water was about to sweep it downriver.

Pearl moved closer to the twosome. "My, my, why, I never would have imagined you two would fancy that little ole watercolor. How odd that you both took to it so."

Katie pried her eyes from the painting to examine Pearl. She found her eyes still piercing, despite the wrinkles that nearly engulfed them. "Why?"

Pearl lifted a thin shoulder and dropped it. "Well, it's simply not that impressive a work to most people. It's by a little-known eighteenth-century Russian painter who died in obscurity."

"And poverty, no doubt?" Blake turned to Katie. "Like most artists."

"Yes, it's hardly fair, is it?"

"Well, this one might have made a living at his work, but he painted so few, even if he had sold them all, he couldn't have supported himself. The ones that survived the revolution are worth quite a bit, however."

Blake glanced at Katie, who knowing what he was thinking, replied with a small nod. "I don't suppose you could part with this one, for the auction?" Charm was layered in his voice, his smile subtly sexy enough to melt a woman's resolve at any age.

"Well, now," Pearl said, eyeing them both specu-

latively, "it seems the two of you are sharing some
private affection—for the painting, that is. I'm sure it
has nothing to do with any more than that, now does
it?"

Katie bristled. So, lunch wasn't the only price today.
If they were to earn their auction donation, they were
going to have to pay with inside information. Which of
course, she wasn't about to dole out.

"Pearl, Blake and I are friends. I don't know what
you've been hearing that might be to the contrary, but
I'm here to tell you it's not true. Isn't that right, Blake?"

Blake nodded, letting Katie's eyes only see his
fingers crossed behind his back. She swallowed the
smile tugging at her mouth.

"Absolutely. Katie and I go way, way back, as you
know. That's why we were both drawn to this painting,
I'm sure. We're kindred spirits of a sort."

"Hmm…" Pearl replied doubtfully. "Well, as I told
ya'll, the final decision is Hal's."

"Now, there's a well-trained woman" came the
booming voice of her Texas oil-magnate husband. Hal
ambled into the library, alligator boots clicking against
mahogany plank floors. "Howdy Blake," he said,
beaming, slapping the younger man's back. Sweeping
his Stetson aside, he bowed to Katie. "Lovelier by the
year. Come on over here and give ole Hal a kiss, girl."

Katie obeyed, knowing Hal to be obnoxious, but
harmless. "Good to see you, Mr. Kennington."

That won her a round of bawdy laughter. "I think
we're long past the Mr. Kennington nonsense, now
aren't we, Katie my girl?"

"I'm sorry. It's my mother's brainwashing."

Pearl cleared her throat to get Hal's attention. "Hal,

they're interested in this little Vladislava work for the auction."

"That scrap? Hell, take it away. You'd be doin' me a favor. Never liked that pathetic little duck hangin' on my library wall anyhow. It's depressin' when I'm sittin' down after a long day with a scotch in one hand and a Cuban in the other. Last thing I want to see is an orphaned kid and a doomed duck starin' at me."

Katie and Blake both laughed. Pearl huffed. "You could have told me and I would have had it moved."

"Wouldn't be worth the grief. Anyhow, take that one and pick out two or three more. I don't give a damn. Got too much stuff in this place anyhow." He waved off the painting. "Now, what I want to know, Miss Katie, is when is that fund-raiser for your uncle Peter? I'll make sure he's the next governor, singlehandedly if I have to."

"He'll be delighted to hear that. It's coming up shortly. I'm sure there's an invitation already in the mail to both of you."

"We can arrange to have the Kenningtons at our table, can't we?"

Katie stared at him. What was Blake doing? Not only did he just give Pearl the best gossip leak she'd get all year, but he was committing them to something she couldn't promise. Was this about the auction items? It couldn't be since Hal had essentially already given them carte blanche. It was as though he wanted to announce he would be her date.

"That would be an honor," Pearl said, hedging. "But I can't imagine you'd be attending that fund-raiser when you McCords have always supported Adam Trent. Will you be escorting Katie?"

"I certainly will."

The touch of pride in his voice was at once complimentary and a little too possessive. Katie was determined to stop the runaway train in Pearl's head before it carried them to disaster. "We're going as friends, just as we've done before to other events."

"Of course, naturally," Blake assured, but she knew him too well to miss the mockery in his tone.

"Sounds like a shindig to me," Hal said jovially. "We'll look forward to hashing over next year's policies and funding at dinner. We oil men gotta keep those regulators under control, know what I mean?"

Blake answered something vague, but Katie was too distracted with her own thoughts to hear it. She managed to move the group along, winding down their other selections and extricating them both from Pearl.

When finally they were off the grounds and on their way to somewhere yet not discussed, she shot Blake a look and let loose with what had been on her mind for over an hour.

"What was that about? I can't promise them a seat at our table!"

"We got five donations, didn't we, including the Russian work?" His tone was too cool, too arrogant. It infuriated her.

She turned in the seat of his car, the leather squeaking under her. "Blake McCord, you know exactly what I'm talking about. You told Pearl deliberately. Why would you do that? You know she's going to be blabbing it to everyone and we're going to get grief even before the fund-raiser. Do you enjoy torture or what?"

"Are you finished?" he asked calmly.

"I'm not sure."

"If you're pausing at least, then I'll explain. The truth

is I can't take being treated like I'm second-best to my little brother. Call me egotistical, but it irritates the hell out of me that everyone still thinks he deserves you more than—than anyone else might. He had his chance and he blew it."

Katie sat in stunned silence. This was not the explanation she'd expected. At all. She'd had no idea Blake felt this way. His seeming possessiveness, his bursts of frustration arose from a sense of inadequacy? That she never would have guessed. Not from Blake. But it touched her somehow, that he cared for her enough to want to be known as someone who was important in her life.

"I didn't realize…"

"I know. And I'm sorry if I was presumptuous in inviting them to your family's table. I just decided it is high time people stop seeing you as my brother's fiancée. You could be with any man you wanted to be with now. And if you choose to go to the fund-raiser or any other event with me, then I consider myself a lucky man and I'm not going to hide that. Gossip or not."

Again, he surprised her, showing a humility she wouldn't have believed he possessed. "Thank you," she said softly, reaching to lay a hand on his arm. "I'm happy you're taking me. To heck with the busybodies."

He smiled over to her. "My sentiments exactly."

His BlackBerry summoned then and with an apologetic glance at her, he answered. From what she could glean, the conversation had to do with McCord jewelry store closings in California. When he hung up he seemed drawn, tired and her heart went out to him.

"Bad news?"

Blake blew out a weary breath. "An omen of things to come, I'm afraid. We've had to close our Boston and

San Diego stores. Unless things turn around soon, this is only the beginning."

"Oh, Blake, I'd heard rumors but I didn't know it had come to this. I'm so sorry."

"Thanks. But I'm not beat yet. I've got a new PR campaign underway and a few other plans in the works. If can pull everything together—"

"I'm sure you will."

"That remains to be seen," he said darkly.

He radiated tension and Katie searched for something to take his mind off business and fund-raisers and gossipy patrons. "We need to find an activity that doesn't involve party planning or politics."

"I might have an idea."

"And that is?"

With a provoking half smile, he turned the Porsche sharply to the right. "Trust me."

In a short while they were on their way up the long, towering pine-tree-lined drive to an exclusive Dallas golf club.

"Golf?" she asked with a laugh.

"Just nine holes. You can still get a couple hours in at the office if you really have to."

"The day is shot. I'll double-time it tomorrow. I didn't know you played golf."

"All work and no play… I'm glad I can still surprise you." He shifted the car to a sharp stop in a premiere parking spot at the formal entry to the club.

"You're surprising me every day lately."

"Good." In one swift move he was out of the car and holding her door open. "Wouldn't want to bore you."

She shook her head. "Not a chance of that."

They strode together beneath the forest-green awning that canopied the entryway. "I don't have clothes," she said, swiping her palms down her tailored suit.

"We can fix that. I have an account in the pro shop."

In no time he and the salesgirl outfitted Katie in an attractive powder-blue golf skirt, white golf shirt, socks, shoes, gloves and hat. They both removed to separate dressing rooms to change and by the time she found him with the caddy, he'd secured her irons and a golf cart.

She caught his approving once-over before she climbed in beside him, noting a bottle of white wine in an icy bucket joined their clubs in the back of the cart.

"You look great."

"Thanks, but fair warning, my golf is somewhere along the lines of my skiing, you know, snow bunny style? I have all of the trappings, but none of the skill."

"We're here for relaxation, not competition. For all I care we can just ride around in this thing and drink wine." With that he stepped on the gas and the cart lurched forward, thrusting Katie nearly out onto the lawn.

"Sorry," he said, taking her arm to right her in her seat. "I drive this thing the way I drive my car. I'll behave, promise."

She laughed. "I didn't know these could go that fast."

"They can't. I had to buy one once because I ruined the engine."

Smiling, she found her tension ebbing. This was a side of Blake she rarely—if ever—had seen. Decidedly, she liked it and secretly hoped to see more of it. The only glitch in enjoying the lighter side of Blake was that it reminded her of Tate. He'd always been the easygoing playboy, the fun one.

"Hey." Blake slowed the cart to a stop beneath a giant old shade tree. "I'm losing you, only this time it's not because you're falling out of the cart."

She swallowed hard. The last thing she wanted to do was to ruin this moment with thoughts of Tate or guilt over being with Blake because of her past with his brother. "No...I'm just enjoying the view," she explained. It was partially true. "That's what I love most about golf courses. They're so scenic, so lush and green. They calm you, you know?"

He nodded. "That's the only reason I even make an attempt to play. Want to give it a go?"

"You first."

They hopped out of the cart, Blake choosing driving irons for them both. Standing behind him, she couldn't help but notice the play of muscle in his back and shoulders as he practiced his swing. Her thoughts wandered in a completely different direction, musing over what it would feel like to run her hands there—

"Well, not too impressive for a first shot. But typical for me." He turned to her. "You're up."

"Hmm? Oh, sure."

"You're really engaged here, I can tell."

She was, but not in the game of golf. She tried to remember the lessons her father had insisted she take in high school, planting her feet the right distance apart, gripping her hands on the club in the right spots, swinging from the back and abs. Still she knew something wasn't right. "I'm hopeless," she said after her first shot dug a nasty hole in the manicured lawn.

"May I?" Blake moved close behind her.

"Please, I need all the help I can get." He pressed

lightly up against her back, wrapping his arms around hers and covering her hands in his.

"Now, just relax and let the feel come naturally," he murmured against her ear.

They swayed together, in a sort of dance that went nowhere. She let her body ease back against his and she could have sworn she heard a slight groan.

"How's that feel?" he asked.

Very nice, she wanted to say. Instead she tried not to sound dizzy and dreamy, the way he made her feel. "It's helping. I think I was just tense."

"Good. Now, let's take one swing together. Ready?"

Letting him do the work, they cracked the iron against the ball and sent it sailing into the air.

"Wow! I can't even see it anymore." Caught up in excitement, she spun and grasped his arm. "That was amazing."

Laughing, he put his hands on her shoulders. "See, you're a natural." His hands lingered, lightly massaging in what felt more like a caress.

"Why is it that I'm feeling like we shouldn't be having so much fun?"

"It's because you're listening to the wrong voices." Gently touching his lips to her forehead, he let his hands slide down her arms to grasp hers. "Try to listen to the one that says it's okay for us to enjoy each other instead of the ones that beat you up for it."

She nodded, knowing he was right, yet wondering if *they* could ever be right.

Chapter Five

A dazzle of lights—the golden glow encompassing the aisle leading to the doorways of the elegant downtown hotel starred with camera flashes—greeted Katie as she took Blake's hand and stepped from the car. There had been no chance they would arrive unnoticed. The fund-raising dinner for Peter Salgar was one of the biggest events of the political season, a glittering display of wealth and power evidenced in the carefully chosen guest list. On name alone, she and Blake were targets for the paparazzi. Tonight especially, with his hand at her waist, his arm lightly pressing against her back in what could easily be construed as a possessive gesture, the stir of interest they created was almost palpable.

Blake seemed oblivious to the ripple of reaction their entrance into the reception area caused among the growing group of guests. "Regrets already?" he murmured close to her ear before they became part of the crowd.

"I should be asking you that question." She stopped, facing him. "I don't think this was such a good idea. You have enough on your mind right now without me adding to it."

"You're not adding to it. I think you know me well enough to be certain I wouldn't be here if I didn't want to be."

"I'm still worried about you," she said, overlooking the clear skepticism, almost disbelief crossing his face. "Rex Foley, and most likely Zane and Jason will be here, too, and—" She shook her head. "I should never have agreed to this."

"We talked about this. It's not as if I'm going to be blindsided. And it's hardly the first time I've been in the same room with the Foleys and I've managed to survive so far." He dismissed her concern but there was a new look in his eyes, almost bemused, as if someone anxious on his behalf was an unfamiliar concept. "Besides, it's too late for you to back out."

"I don't want to back out, but I wouldn't blame you if you did."

"That's the last thing on my mind right now." Blake reached to her and lightly dragged his fingertips over her cheek, his eyes following the motion then quickly sweeping over her. "You're so beautiful, Katie. And in that dress…" His open admiration made her glad that on impulse she'd forgone her usual black for a deep red, in a style slightly less conservative than her custom. "Tate was an idiot to ever let you go."

The husky note in his voice momentarily disarmed her fears. He was distractingly attractive, the black-and-white formal attire accentuating his lean good looks, but times like this, when he gave her a glimpse of warmth and charm behind his cool exterior, were when she found him most irresistible.

They might have been alone in those brief seconds. His gaze, with its now familiar intensity, held hers and she had the disconcerting sensation of falling. That was a novel experience for her. That Blake was the cause made it all the more unsettling.

How it would have ended if it had remained only the two of them, she never knew, because her parents chose that moment to interrupt, breaking the fleeting communion between her and Blake.

"Katerina, there you are." Anna and Benton Salgar walked up to them and though their timing frustrated Katie, she made herself smile. Still a beauty in diamonds and a shimmering silver gown, Anna's seemingly effortless elegance and her greeting to her daughter—a brief clasping of hands and touch of cheeks—were marred by her slight frown as she recognized Katie's companion. "We didn't expect to see you here, Blake. This is quite a surprise."

"Peter will be happy if you've switched sides," Benton said as he shook Blake's hand. "He didn't think he had a chance at an endorsement from the McCords. We assumed Eleanor would continue to back Adam."

"I assume she will, as well," Blake answered. "I'm not representing my family. I'm here for Katie."

"Blake offered to escort me tonight," Katie intervened hurriedly at the surprised looks her parents alternated between her and Blake.

Benton and Anna exchanged a glance before he said,

"You didn't mention that when you turned down coming with us."

"It's no wonder people are talking," Anna said, sounding irritated as she focused on Katie.

"That's going to happen no matter what I do."

"Well, you must admit, it's odd, you two being seen together this often and so soon after you and Tate broke your engagement."

"There's nothing odd about attending a party with a friend." Turning to Blake, Katie put a hand on his arm. "I'd love a glass of wine. Will you come with me?" As soon as they'd excused themselves and were out of earshot of Anna and Benton, she told him, "I'm sorry for that. My parents still haven't given up on the idea Tate and I might get back together. Apparently his new fiancée isn't enough to convince them it's well and truly over."

Blake's face gave nothing of his feelings away. He didn't answer until they'd made their way to the bar and he'd given their orders. "Why do I get the impression that in their eyes, I'm partly to blame for your breakup?"

"They don't. At least …" She accepted the wine glass he offered her, flushing at his outright incredulity. "As my mother said, people talk. We've spent a lot of time together since the Labor Day party and although it's mostly been because of the hospital, you know as well as I do there are some people who just wait to pounce on anything appearing even remotely scandalous. After that fiasco with Pearl, you should have guessed the gossip was only going to get worse."

He ignored the reference to the Kenningtons. "Is that what we are, Katie," he said, the low, suggestive undertone in his voice sending a pleasant shiver through her, "remotely scandalous?"

She could have taken him seriously, fretted over the image they made in a very public setting, questioned her judgment in getting entangled with him to the extent she had when she was trying to find her way after Tate. Instead, she chose to toss him a half smile and to enjoy the surprise that touched his expression. "Probably. Does it bother you?"

"For the most part, no."

Remembering again his forceful assertion that he would never be second-best to Tate or anyone else, Katie guessed that was what bothered him the most about the evening. She also knew he'd deny it if she confronted him. She could consider it arrogance on his part and refuse to pander to his ego. Yet, it was a vulnerability that struck a chord in her because she'd never imagined Blake as anything but completely sure of himself and his abilities and disdainful of anyone who thought otherwise.

"Maybe I'll let them believe it," she said on sudden impulse.

"Believe what?"

"That you're to blame for my being unattached. Who knows—" she teased him a bit "—for a change, a little scandal might be fun."

"If I thought you were serious—"

"Who says I'm not?" He frowned and she laughed. "Oh, for heaven's sake, Blake, of course I'm not serious. You'd never forgive me."

"That depends," he said as he moved a step closer, very nearly crossing the line from polite into personal space, "on whether or not you meant it."

She suddenly lost control of the game she'd started. He was asking her something she couldn't answer, not yet, when she wasn't ready to redefine how she felt about him. "If I did something of that magnitude," she said, forcing a lightness she didn't feel, "I would mean it."

Blake didn't respond in kind; if anything he looked even more troubled. "I think you would," he said slowly.

"Is it that hard for you to believe that I care about your feelings?" That it apparently was difficult for him made her wonder if anyone else ever had. Abandoning her wineglass, she put a hand on his shoulder and brushed a kiss against his cheek. "Thank you for being here. You're the only man I've ever known who would put himself through this for me."

"You don't need to thank me for something I wanted to do," he said gruffly, then, unbending for her, he briefly touched her hand. "You're welcome." They looked at each other and he gave her that half smile of his. "I guess this means we're both staying."

"I guess it does," she said, returning a smile of her own. "Who knows, we might even find something to enjoy before it's over."

"That," Blake said, taking her hand and fitting it into the curve of his arm, "I can promise you."

Blake found it difficult to keep that promise through dinner and speech-making and the hour of headline entertainment that followed. He and Katie were seated at the head table with Peter Salgar, his family, the Kenningtons and Katie's parents, a less than comfortable arrangement. Peter took advantage of Blake's unexpected presence and what he apparently assumed was Blake's attachment to Katie to subtly lobby for Blake's support. Benton and Anna, though making an effort to be pleasant, couldn't completely mask their disapproval of Katie's choice of companion; and more than once,

Blake felt eyes on his back from Rex Foley and his two oldest sons, Zane and Jason, sitting at the neighboring table. If it hadn't been for Katie, he would have told the lot of them to go to hell and been done with it.

"Blake…?"

His name, a softly spoken question, pulled him out of his thoughts and he found himself alone at the table with Katie and looking into her dark eyes.

"For a moment there, I thought I'd lost you," she said, smiling a little.

"I'm sorry, I let myself get distracted."

"That's not very flattering."

"It's just been one of those long evenings. It isn't you."

"You're not very good for my ego, you know." She glanced to their right, where the Foley men were getting to their feet, Zane and his beautiful blonde companion leaving them to join other couples who were moving to the open ballroom floor for the start of the dancing. "I was hoping I could talk you into at least one dance. But I'm sure I can find another partner. Jason Foley, maybe. Considering his reputation and the way he always eyes practically every woman in the room, I doubt I'd have difficulty convincing him."

"If that son of a bitch so much as—" Blake started, breaking off when her lips twitched with suppressed laughter and he realized she was messing with him. "Not nice, Katie."

"It got your attention, though."

"I assure you, you have my attention." He moved his hand to the back of her chair until his fingers slid against the smooth bare skin exposed by the low dip of her dress. "As much of it as you want."

The faint rise of color in her cheeks and her quick

intake of breath betrayed her attempt to appear unaffected by his touch. "I'll need proof of that."

"Then dance with me."

She accepted his invitation by taking his proffered hand and standing with him, her eyes never leaving his.

Their path to the dance floor took them directly past the Foleys' table and though Blake preferred to avoid acknowledging them, Rex Foley made that impossible by stepping up to them. Jason, he noted, hung back, watching them from a few feet away.

"It's nice to see you again, Katie," Rex said, the smile he gave her coming easily, as if to an old friend. "I know Peter appreciates you being here."

"And he appreciates your support. He always has," Katie answered. Her swift sidelong glance his way told Blake she keenly felt the awkwardness of the meeting. "It means a lot to him."

Rex nodded, then looked to Blake. "You being here is a surprise."

"So I've been told, numerous times," Blake retorted coldly.

"I know Eleanor—" Rex gave her name soft edges "—still backs Adam Trent. That puts you in the enemy camp, so to speak, at least tonight."

"I don't always agree with my mother's choices of friends." *Or lovers*, he nearly added but held his tongue. His mother's relationship, past and present, with Rex Foley was the last thing he wanted to get into right now or at all, for that matter. "And my reasons for being here are my business."

From his look between Blake and Katie, it was obvious Rex had formed his own idea of why Blake was here but he only nodded. "I'm sure Eleanor understands." He seemed about to add something but left it unsaid.

"I'm beyond the age of needing her approval. Now, if you'll excuse us—" He didn't wait for Rex's reply but with his hand to her back, gently urged Katie forward.

"That could have been worse," Katie ventured a few moments later. "At least Jason didn't get involved."

"For good reason," Blake said shortly. "He and Penny are apparently seeing each other. He's probably not sure how much I know about it and isn't interested in hearing my opinion."

"Penny? Your sister Penny is *dating* Jason Foley?"

"That's what she calls it. But I doubt he sees it that way."

"I have a hard time believing Jason and Penny—" Katie broke off with a rueful grimace. "I'm sorry, that didn't come out the way I meant it."

"It's okay, I have a hard time believing it, too." Penny was her twin sister Paige's opposite, quiet and shy, hardly the type to be attracted to a brash womanizer like Jason Foley. She wasn't his type, either. "I'm certain Jason is trying to use Penny to get any scrap of information he can about my plans for McCord Jewelers. I just can't convince her of that."

"You could be right," Katie said slowly. "But that's between her and Jason."

They stopped short of the dance floor, facing each other. "If you're telling me to butt out, I can't. Not when it involves my business."

"Give Penny some credit. I doubt she's going to betray any family secrets. I'm sure you hate the idea of anyone in your family in a relationship with a Foley, but Penny has to make her own choices, without your interference."

"I thought you'd be on my side with this."

Katie sighed. "It's not about taking sides, Blake. I understand what it's like to have families meddling in your relationships. Look at Tate and me. I grew up never having to decide for myself what I wanted in a lover or a husband because our families told us we were perfect for each other. Now I have no clue what I want or need or how to have a relationship with someone who isn't Tate. I wouldn't wish that on Penny or anyone else."

"Even if you knew she was making a big mistake?" Blake shot back.

"Even then. It's her mistake to make." Catching her bottom lip between her teeth, Katie hesitated then touched his arm. "I know you think you know best, but this is one time you have to let someone else deal with the situation. If you keep trying to interfere, you're only going to make things worse."

He didn't want to admit she could be right. His mistrust of the Foleys was too ingrained, and Penny's involvement with Jason Foley seemed almost as much of a betrayal as his mother's affair with Rex. "I see your point," he finally conceded.

"But—?"

"But I don't know that I agree."

"At least promise me you'll think about it."

"I promise," he said, unable to deny her appeal with her so close and looking into his eyes. Then she smiled and he knew he was lost. He held out his hand to her. "You promised me a dance."

A new melody started, slow and sensual. As he took her in his arms she yielded, malleable to his touch and the rhythm of the music. Somewhere, at the edge of perception, Blake could hear it, feel the brush and heat of other bodies, but it all seemed removed, as if time had caught them in a suspended moment.

He became very aware of how close he held her, how her hand curved against his shoulder, the other clasped in his. Of how, with her dark hair framing her face, in a dress that shaped her curves, and the movement around them shifting shadow and light against the ivory of her skin, she looked like his fantasies personified. And that, with the slightest motion, a simple slide of hands and bodies, the tensions between them would twist into a different fire that had nothing to do with the evening's frustrations.

Sliding his arm further around her waist, he pressed her closer, his cheek against the silk of her hair, and she leaned slightly nearer, her breath brushing the hollow of his throat. Their coming together wasn't a conscious thing on his part, or it seemed hers, and the fact they didn't seem to have any control over it made it all the more bewildering.

The music came to an end on a soulful, lingering note, leaving them looking at each other for seconds—minutes? hours?—while the other couples moved around them, and the band began another song.

Katie's lips parted but nothing came out and Blake had a pretty fair idea of how she felt. They'd started something but, like her, and for the first time, he didn't have a clue what was supposed to happen next.

"We should go back and mingle, or I should at least," she said finally.

"We should," he agreed, though he made no move to let her go.

"Uncle Peter and my parents will be wondering where I am."

"Probably."

The music wove around them and she shifted closer again. "You're becoming a bad influence."

"Me?" They swayed together and Blake's attention fixed on Katie, making him ignore everything else. "No one's ever accused me of that before."

"Yes, you, and your 'do things your way and to hell with what anyone else thinks' attitude."

"I was in trouble for that a little while ago," he reminded her.

"That was different. Here and now, I like it."

"Maybe you should try it yourself more often."

"Maybe I should," she echoed softly. "Who knows what might happen?"

Blake didn't have an answer so he simply held her, and for a little while, that was all that mattered.

Chapter Six

Blake didn't need to be told there were repercussions from his night with Katie; one look at his mother, Paige and Tate's faces when he walked into the dining room the next evening said everything. He'd managed to avoid any confrontation up until now by leaving the house before breakfast, but that was only a delaying tactic.

Forgoing any usual greetings, Eleanor held out a newspaper section to him, turned to a story on Peter Salgar's fund-raising efforts. The report was accompanied by a photo of Peter and his wife in conversation with a congressman and a high-profile attorney, Katie and Blake standing to the side. "This was an interesting way to start the day. Adam called me to ask what it meant and I had no idea how to answer him. If you were going to put yourself in a position of appearing to support Peter Salgar, I would have appreciated an advance warning."

"It looks more like he's supporting Katie," Paige commented, directing the attention away from politics to a potentially more dangerous topic. She darted a quick grin at Blake, not in the least quelled by the scowl he returned. "What's going on between you two, anyway?"

"Nothing that you're imagining," Blake said, unable to keep his irritation from showing. "We're friends. She needed an escort. I volunteered."

"Yes, that—" Paige gestured to the newspaper photo "—looks very *friendly*."

Blake silently admitted that their pose—his hand curved around Katie's waist, her leaning slightly into his arm—suggested they were closer than friends. It was his expression, though, that clearly betrayed him. The photographer had caught him in an unguarded moment, his eyes on Katie as she smiled at her uncle, and even he recognized the desire and what, in another man, he might have even called tenderness.

Giving the photograph a brief appraisal, Eleanor turned a watchful gaze on Blake. "You and Katie have been spending quite a lot of time together. Do you think that's wise, considering the circumstances?"

"What *circumstances* would those be?"

"The timing—" Eleanor glanced to Tate.

"Doesn't matter," Tate interrupted. "No one can accuse Blake of taking Katie away from me."

"Or of cheating on someone else," Paige muttered darkly.

Eleanor's face constricted but she said nothing in response to her daughter's not-so-subtle reference to her affair with Rex Foley. Paige, like Blake, hadn't made much of an attempt to hide her resentment of what both of them considered Eleanor's betrayal.

"I hate to spoil the perception of drama, but every-one's making much more of this than it was." Blake kept his voice level. "I didn't declare my undying loyalty to Peter Salgar, and Katie and I aren't a couple." No one at the table looked convinced, prompting Blake to deliberately change the subject before he lost his temper and told his family to mind their own business. "Where's Penny tonight? I expected she'd be here."

"She said she was going out," Eleanor said carefully, not quite meeting his eyes.

"Meaning she's seeing Jason Foley."

"I don't know that for certain. But it's likely. She refuses to talk about it with anyone. And it's no use you stating the obvious, that you don't approve." Eleanor went ahead before Blake could say anything. "I'm not sure I do, either. But Penny's a grown woman. None of us can make her choices for her."

It was essentially the same thing Katie had said to him. He didn't like hearing it any more now than he had then. But it was remembering Katie asking him to stay out of it that kept him from arguing his opinion that Jason Foley was using Penny.

It was a relief, less than an hour later, to escape the strained atmosphere that pervaded the remainder of dinner. Blake was on his way to the study, intent on checking some e-mails, when Tate stopped him.

"I hope you know I meant what I said," Tate told him.

"I know it. And—thanks." He and Tate had heatedly argued more than once in recent weeks, mostly over Katie, but Blake appreciated his brother's support.

"I also hope you know what you're doing."

"I always know what I'm doing."

"With business, and probably with any other woman you've known. But Katie is different."

"I don't need you telling me that," Blake snapped, suddenly angry. "I've been telling you all along how special she is. You're the one who let her go."

Tate surprised him by not responding in kind. Instead he studied Blake for a moment before saying, "I don't think you do know what you're doing this time."

"I'm not interested in your opinion."

"Probably not. But I don't want Katie to get hurt."

"And the assumption is I'm going to do that?" The implication stung because Blake knew he could easily do that. He'd never committed himself to any relationship. His expectations with women were as high as his certainty that he would end up disappointed, and consequently he refused to let himself get more than superficially involved. But, irrationally it seemed, he still resented Tate automatically deciding Blake's involvement with Katie would end badly.

"I didn't say that." An aggravated note worked its way into Tate's voice. "I'm just saying to be careful with her."

"Like you were?"

Tate blew out a breath. "I don't want to get into this with you again. We've done it enough over the past few weeks and it's getting old. I'll just add one thing—if this is your way of proving, once again, that you're the best man for the job, then get out now. Like you keep telling me, Katie deserves better."

Not giving Blake time to counter him, Tate swiftly turned and strode away, leaving Blake alone with the unwelcome thought that when it came to him and Katie, his brother might be right.

* * *

In the middle of the majestic ballroom, the sunlight dancing stars on the crystal of the chandeliers set in the high ceiling, Katie half listened to the woman detailing the amenities of the room. The woman's voice was slowly becoming a background drone as Katie's attention kept wandering as she tried to figure out Blake's mood.

He'd agreed readily enough to accompany her here, to the historic music hall where the Halloween ball would be held, to settle some details about the event and the location of various activities within the hall itself. But he'd been tense and withdrawn, cold almost, so very different from the man who two days ago had danced with her, held her close, looked at her in a way that had stirred to life desires she'd barely recognized.

Her name and the words *wine tasting* penetrated her distraction and she gave a slight start, realizing she'd completely missed the last few minutes of conversation.

"I'm sorry," she said hastily, avoiding Blake's sardonic glance in favor of the woman's slightly affronted face, "I let myself get sidetracked imagining how lovely a setting this is going to be for the ball. A wine tasting would be wonderful."

The woman beamed, mollified by Katie's explanation and her apologetic smile. "If you don't mind waiting a few minutes, I'll get that set up for you."

"Lovely, is it?" Blake asked after the woman had gone. He glanced around them, frowning as if he was inspecting the ballroom and it had fallen short of his expectations.

"Yes, it is. Which is more than I can say for your mood," Katie said before she could stop herself. "If you didn't want to do this today, you should have said so. I could have handled it myself."

He stared at her a moment then shook his head and for the first time in the last hour appeared to relax. "So you could have. But I wanted to be here to help. We're supposed to be a team."

"*Supposed* to be…?"

"Okay, we're a team."

"Mmm…considering how much you dislike the whole idea of depending on someone else, that must have hurt to admit."

"A little."

She smiled and drew an answering half smile from Blake.

"Now if you're through forcing me to inflict pain on myself," he said, "maybe you can explain again how we're going to manage nearly a thousand people, a string ensemble, and all these activities in this one *lovely* ballroom."

"There's plenty of room," she assured him. Laying a hand on his arm, she directed his attention upward. "We'll have all the balcony space, as well as the ballroom, and there's seating and standing space just outside by the bar—" Katie broke off when she realized he wasn't following her gestures but watching her face. Her breath hitched and the room suddenly felt warmer but she tried to hang on to her composure. "Don't ask for explanations if you aren't going to listen."

"Balcony, ballroom, outside by the bar," he repeated. He took a step closer and slowly ran his hand over her shoulder and up the curve of her throat until his fingers threaded into her hair. "Got it."

She didn't doubt it but when he leaned in to kiss her she didn't care. Ballrooms, space and wine retreated and she yielded to what she wanted—uncaring of where they were, no space between them, reveling in the taste of him. Maybe it wasn't wise, as everyone around them kept reminding her, but reason had nothing to do with the electric feelings that sprang up between them every time they got within touching distance. Blake didn't deny them, either, forgoing any gentle, exploratory caress and kissing her deeply, pulling her closer when she wrapped her arms around his neck and urged him in that direction.

"We're ready for—oh." The woman's voice broke them apart, although Blake didn't quite release her. "The wine tasting…we're ready—if you…" Waving her hand in the general direction of the door, the woman avoided looking directly at them.

Katie bit her lip against laughing, caught the amusement in Blake's eyes, and had to glance away from him for fear it would burst out anyway.

"We probably shouldn't be doing this before lunch," she murmured half an hour later, when they were nearly finished sampling the array of wines and deciding which they wanted available at the ball.

"Worried you'll get tipsy and I'll take advantage of you?" Blake asked as he leaned back in his chair, eyeing the sample of burgundy he was trying.

"You do that without the benefit of wine," she lightly accused. "And who says it wouldn't be the other way around?"

His brow lifted slightly. "I promise not to object."

"I'll keep that in mind." Annoyed at the warmth that crept over her throat and face, Katie glanced at their checklist. "We just need to decide on the champagne and then we're done."

"You're on your own there."

"You can't tell me you don't like champagne." She affected to look shocked at his shrug. "I don't see how that's possible. Some of my favorite fantasies involve it."

She'd definitely gotten his attention with that one. He straightened, a now familiar glint in his eyes. "Would you care to elaborate?"

"No," she said, laughing, "you'll have to be satisfied with imagining."

"That could be dangerous. I can imagine quite a bit."

"Really? I never took you for the creative type, Blake."

"If you'd like a demonstration—"

Katie studied the list a moment before checking off a selection of sparkling wines she was familiar with and then got to her feet. "Not here. I think we've embarrassed the staff enough for one day. And I really am ready for lunch."

"Then I'll take you to lunch," Blake said, rising with her.

"How about I take you?" She was pleased at being able to surprise him with the offer, pleased overall with the light, flirtatious mood between them, a welcome change from that morning. "It's Saturday, the sun is shining and I don't feel like anything fussy. I have just the place in mind."

"Then I'll let you lead the way."

"You will?"

Putting his arm around her waist, Blake brushed his mouth against her temple and murmured, "Just this once."

Katie chose a small, quaint café on a quiet backstreet that she'd stumbled upon one time when searching out a specialty shop in the area. It was a distance from her and Blake's usual haunts—the elegant, expensive restaurants and upscale nightclubs—and they were unlikely to run into anyone they knew, the reason she liked it best.

"This was a good choice," Blake said, settling back in his chair after they'd given their orders.

"You like it?"

He smiled a little. "You sound surprised. Yes, I do like it. It feels like an escape."

"That's exactly how I feel, too. I've always come here alone for that reason," she added.

"Ah, so you don't like to share. How did I rate an invitation?"

"I thought you, of anybody, would appreciate it." She paused for a moment then said, "Everything is so serious with you. You take so much on and you're always pushing yourself. And now all this pressure with your business—if anyone needs a break, it's you. You should do it more often, or in your case, do it period."

"I'm starting to feel like one of your charity projects," he said, but without his usual sardonic sting. "Aren't you busy enough without adding me to the list?"

"Probably, but I can never resist a good challenge."

That made him laugh, and Katie liked the way it changed him. In this setting, forgetting work and responsibility for a while, he looked younger, more at ease, definitely more approachable, and at his most appealing.

"So is this your only way of escaping," Blake asked about halfway through lunch, "or do you have others? Something involving champagne, maybe?"

"You might as well give up. I'm not going to tell you," she insisted. Though with the right persuasion on his part—Katie quashed that thought immediately and hoped the warm rush the idea caused hadn't translated into a telltale blush. "I do have a few others."

"Should I assume they involve shopping or the spa?"

"You should not. You obviously need to change your ideas about what women like."

The expression in his eyes suggested he had several ideas and this time she didn't have to wonder about the blush. "Tell me what you like, Katie."

"I don't think you'd be interested," she said, avoiding looking at him.

"You might be surprised. Come on," Blake coaxed, "tell me one thing, one of your favorites."

"All right, one thing." She considered for a moment. "This is a little silly…"

"I doubt it, but I promise not to laugh."

"Okay, I love Bogart movies. Occasionally, I lock myself in the den with a week's supply of popcorn and spend the night watching my favorites." Feeling slightly self-conscious at her admission, she added, "I've never told anyone else that, so I'm counting on you to keep my secret."

Blake reached out and took her hand, threading her fingers with his. "You can count on me, Katie." And it sounded almost like a vow that had nothing to do with her penchant for old movies. "I promise."

One thing she knew for certain about Blake McCord, he didn't take his promises lightly and knowing he intended to keep this one caused a mixed up mess of pleasure, confusion, desire and uncertainty in her that Katie couldn't begin to sort out.

She didn't try, not now, but allowed herself to enjoy being with him, here in this temporary haven, where nothing and no one else intruded, and to believe it could be the beginning of something she had never expected.

Chapter Seven

"Katerina, it's only for the weekend." Anna Salgar's growing frustration with her daughter was clear as she slapped smooth hands to slender hips. "You need a dress for the ball and I won't have you attending in something from Dallas. It's too risky."

Katie groaned. "Oh, Mother, don't be ridiculous. There are dozens of designer stores here. I'll find something no one else would *dare* wear. I promise."

"That's not what I mean and you know it." Anna turned her back and idly fingered an Italian jewelry box on Katie's bureau. "Tate brought this to you, didn't he? From Florence?"

"Yes, and—"

Anna opened the box listened to a chimed rendition of Tchaikovsky's *The Sleeping Beauty* waltz, closed the box and faced her daughter. "And, since you keep telling me that you and Tate are finished, that means you're single and available. You can't take chances with your attire. You need to dress appropriately and with a singular sense of style."

Katie paced in front of the floor-to-ceiling windows at the back of her bedroom suite. *Single, what is that?* For as long as she could remember she'd been promised to, then engaged to Tate. She dropped down on the edge of her bed and let her face sink into her palms, forgetting any pretense of grace. "Mother, I don't even know what that means."

"Oh, darling, I know," Anna said, moving to sit next to her. "That's why I want to take you to New York, just the two of us, for a mother-daughter shopping trip. I need to show you how to enjoy your new freedom." She brushed a lock of hair from Katie's cheek. "I never imagined you'd face this day, but you have and now we have to switch strategies."

Katie's chin went up. "Strategies?"

"Well, perhaps that's a poor choice of words, but what I mean is that you have to learn new skills, have a new attitude toward men. And yourself."

Thoughts of Blake rose in her mind. She wasn't *with* Blake as a lover, but there was no denying they'd become more than friends. She felt lost, confused, as though in a no-man's-land. Should she heed her mother's advice? It felt that's what she'd always been doing when it came to her relationship with Tate, listening to what others told her was best, never considering if it was what she wanted.

Yet here she was, over thirty and for the first time in her life single. How did one be single, anyhow?

"This sounds ridiculous at my age, but honestly,

Mom, I'm afraid I don't know what the rules are and I'm not sure I really want to learn."

"Of course you do. And I want to help you with all of that. It's important now that you're no longer engaged, that you don't rush into anything—or anyone—else."

Anna's implication was clear, though Katie knew well her mother would far rather avoid a confrontation over Blake, relying instead on understatement and implication than actual honesty, than tell her straight-out to keep her distance from another McCord man.

"That isn't a problem," she said flatly, trying to ease her mother's suspicions.

It was a problem, though. *He* was a problem. She couldn't stop thinking about him, about the time they'd enjoyed together recently, about how comfortable she felt with him. How much she wanted more...

"Good," Anna said, obviously relieved. She patted Katie's leg then stood and strode over to open the double doors to Katie's expansive walk-in closet. "We may need to start from scratch," she said, fingering dress after dress, blouse after blouse, skirt after skirt, her expression mostly disapproving.

Katie followed her. "I like my clothes."

"You have wonderful taste, dear, but we may have to, well, tweak it."

Shaking her head, knowing if she didn't put a stop to it here and now, Anna would take over her closet *and* her love life. "Okay, let's compromise. I'll go to New York to buy a dress for the ball, but only if you promise not to throw out one piece of clothing from my closet until we can talk more about this and go over things together."

Considering, Anna slowed her rapid-fire sweep of Katie's clothing, shoes, purses, belts, scarves. Anna was on a mission now and it frightened Katie. Her mother's will was harder than any diamond in the McCord collection. Anna lingered over a black cashmere sweaterdress, weighing the quality of the fabric between her index finger and thumb.

Katie held her breath and her stance. She wasn't going to give in to her mother this time.

Finally, Anna dropped the piece of fabric and turned to Katie with a conservative smile. "So, we'll start with New York."

Katie's arms were so loaded down with bags when her cell phone rang that she had to drop several of them smack onto the Fifth Avenue sidewalk to grab her phone.

Anna had stopped alongside her, but discouraged her from answering the phone. "Let it go. You can get the message later."

"I can't. It might be Blake." His name spilled out unchecked and she hurried to find an explanation. "We're right in the middle of finalizing auction items. He might need information."

"Hmm" was all Anna would reply.

"Finally." Katie jerked her phone from the bottom of her purse and flipped it open. "Hello," she said breathlessly, the brilliant sunlight overhead preventing her from reading the name on the screen.

"You sound more like you're at the gym than a boutique."

It's Blake, thank heavens, she mused. The New York trip had come up so suddenly she'd only had time to say goodbye over the phone, in a message no less. Because they hadn't spoken she wondered if he might think she was running away, or that she needed a break from him.

"Katie, are you there? All I hear is heavy breathing. Not that, given the right circumstances, that's a bad thing."

Oh, yes, that's what she needed right now, on a busy street, with her mother hanging on her every word—Blake being suggestive. "Um, yes, sorry. We're in the middle of foot traffic on Fifth Avenue. My arms are loaded down and I couldn't find my cell."

"So, it's been a productive venture?"

"Far too much so." Katie glanced at Anna, who huddled her chinchilla coat around herself. "Mother bought out three boutiques."

"I thought you went for one dress."

"Me, too." She heard his deep laughter resonate at the other end and suddenly ached to see the smile that went with it. "I think I've been hijacked."

Though her mother wore oversize sunglasses, Katie knew she was rolling her eyes behind them.

"So how are things there? Any news on those last few donations?" They were hardly the questions she wanted to ask but under the circumstances had little choice. She was tempted to ask him if he missed her, if he'd thought about her as much as she'd thought about him. Spoken in her mind, though, those queries sounded a bit childish, a demand for reassurances he couldn't give.

There was a long silence and then "I miss you."

Her heart jumped. Anna's big black shades were riveted on her. "Yes, exactly, my thoughts exactly."

Again the familiar amusement in his voice. "If I didn't want to see you so much, it would be fun to know you're standing there in the heart of the Big Apple squirming."

"You can be an arrogant jerk, you know that?"

"Yes. But I still miss you."

"Katie, I'm freezing. Can you please continue this little tête-à-tête indoors?" Anna flagged a cab. "Let's go over to the Plaza for a hot toddy."

She nodded to her mother. "Can I call you later? Mother is cold and we need to catch a cab."

"I'll be here. I just wanted talk for a moment. Your message was a poor substitute."

Katie felt a twist in her chest, something between thrilled and frustrated. "It helped me, too."

"Ring whenever you're free, okay?"

"Tonight, um, after—"

"After your mother is asleep?"

"Exactly," she said with a slightly guilty schoolgirl laugh.

"Have fun."

"Thanks. I'll try." She wanted to add that it would be much easier if he were there with her, but instead settled for a soft goodbye.

An hour later, warm and comfortably cozy in their corner of the vast and recently renovated Park Plaza bar area, Katie stared out a giant picture window toward Central Park. At certain angles she could catch glimpses of horses and carriages, couples nestled beneath blankets, enjoying the crisp late autumn air and the golden reflection of waning sunlight—enjoying each other.

She knew it was corny, and Blake would probably laugh at her, but somehow she'd always imagined a horse and carriage ride through Central Park on a starry eve to be hopelessly romantic. Would he even be able to sit still for an hour's ride? So driven, so ambitious and responsible, would he be on edge and miss the wonder of the entire experience?

"If I wanted to keep myself company, I would have come to New York alone."

Katie looked up to where her mother was reseating herself, not even realizing she must have left for the ladies' room. "I'm sorry. I have a lot on my mind right now with the ball and so on. I let myself get distracted."

Anna lifted a crystal champagne glass, pink from the Kir Royal filling it. She must have switched from toddies to champagne when cocktail hour started. Something else Katie had failed to notice.

"Liar."

Katie jerked back. "Excuse me?"

"You've been *distracted* since Blake called."

Sipping her now icy cold hot toddy, Katie winced. "You're jumping to conclusions."

"You expect me to believe you haven't been thinking about him the whole time?" When Katie answered with an exasperated shake of her head, Anna flashed a bright smile that was as false as Katie's denial. "Well, if that's true, then you won't mind entertaining one of New York's premiere residents."

Katie sighed. Her mother was up to something; she'd sensed it from the start but tried to believe it wasn't so. Inwardly counting to ten to calm her anger, she took a deep, soothing breath then confronted Anna. "What are you talking about? I thought this was a girls' weekend."

"Oh, it is, it is, darling. I just thought it might be fun to have a drink—and perhaps dinner—with an old friend's son."

"I can't believe you," Katie groaned. "Please tell me you didn't bring me here to try to set me up."

"How suspicious you are! Oh, there he is—" She shook a warning red-nailed finger. "Now you be nice."

Gritting her teeth, Katie followed her mother's eyes to a tall, dark and attractive man wearing a designer suit cut and sewn to every lean line of his towering frame. He strode toward them with the ease of a man who might well have lived at the Park Plaza. Smiling broadly, a waiter rushed over to him and the taller man bent to give an order in his ear. Before Katie could get up and beat a hasty exit he was there, standing over them, grinning.

"Hello, Anna, stunning as ever," he said smoothly, reaching to brush a kiss to Anna's hand. "And you must be Katerina," he said with a slight bow and an ever-so-subtle sweep of a gaze.

"Katie," she managed as politely as possible.

"Katie, this is Ruth's son, Girard. Remember, Ruth is one of my dearest friends from Wellesley. We were in the same sorority and have been friends ever since."

"It's just a shame you two live so far apart," Girard said, "and that Mother isn't up to traveling these days."

"It is a shame. I'd loved to have seen her. I'll fly up east again this summer for a visit. Dallas is unbearable in July. Oh, my, I'm so sorry, please, do sit down. We've a chair right here."

Reluctantly, Katie scooted away from her window enough to allow him access to the chair next to her. Her mother had thought of everything, even in her choice of table and seating. Typical. She tried to reason that her mother wanted only what she thought was best for her, but after getting past Tate, already Anna was again interfering in her choices in men and in life. It was all Katie could do not to take her irritation out on Girard.

He was catching Anna up on his mother's health when the waiter arrived with a bottle of French wine and a tray of elegant appetizers. He turned to Katie. "I hope you don't mind. I just finished a rough day on Wall Street and I could use a drink and a snack. If you don't like the wine, I'll get another."

"It all looks lovely," Katie said, hoping no sarcasm slipped into her tone. The spread was lovely, the wine was lovely, Girard was lovely, but she wasn't so lovely. She felt quite unlovely actually, since all she wanted to do was to get away from all of this loveliness and go home to Blake. Who at times wasn't so lovely. But somehow, most of the time at least, instinctively, she understood why.

"It looks like your shopping trip has been a success," Girard mentioned, smiling over the heap of elegant shopping bags stacked around them.

"Oh, yes, we've found the perfect dress for the charity ball Katie is organizing. It's simply smashing, made for her. Take it out and show him, Katie."

"No, really, I don't think so," Katie said, trying not to grit her teeth. "This isn't the place."

Girard laid a gentle hand on her shoulder. "I'll take your mother's word for it. What color is it?"

"Midnight-blue," she said softly, managing not to flinch when he touched her, though she found the sensation oddly disconcerting. She realized she didn't want him or any man other than Blake to touch her. When had that happened? Throughout her relationship with Tate, she'd danced with other men, allowed them to put an arm around her now and then, even held a hand or two or accepted a kiss here and there. It had meant nothing. Now she felt a sense of betrayal. It was irrational and ridiculous, yet in an odd sort of way it felt good to know she cared enough about one man not to want the attentions of another.

"It sounds perfect," he was saying.

She thanked him politely and changed the subject.

They chatted pleasantly enough and by the time they'd finished their wine and appetizers, he'd succeeded in convincing them to go to a quaint but elegant Italian restaurant where they worked their way through four courses and a couple more bottles of fabulous Italian wine. When he escorted them back to their hotel, Anna excused herself to the elevator, leaving Katie to say a sleepy and a bit tipsy good-night.

"May I see you again?" Girard asked as he walked slowly beside her to the elevator. It opened, the doorman waiting patiently inside.

"Thank you, but I—" *I'm what? Involved with my ex-fiancé's brother?*

"No problem." He lifted a finger to her lips. "I don't need an explanation." He extended a hand kindly, but with an air of distance. "It was a pleasure to have met you. I hope the remainder of your visit is wonderful. If you need anything at all, your mother knows how to reach me." With a tip for the elevator operator and a gentlemanly nod, he turned on his heel and headed across the marble lobby to the front door.

She watched him walk away, not wishing to follow or that he would come back, but wondering for the first time if what her mother had said had some truth to it. Was she rushing into something with Blake? Should she take more time exploring being single and dating other men before she made up her mind what she wanted?

Logic and reason gave her a definite yes. But her heart stayed silent, steady, Blake's name echoing on every beat.

Chapter Eight

Katie rubbed at her temple, feeling the threat of a headache. "Is there some reason why these grant applications have to be six-dozen pages long?" she grumbled.

Looking up from her notes, Tessa grinned. "I'm sure it's nothing personal."

"Right now, it seems like it. I feel like we've been working on this same paperwork for weeks." She sighed, put aside her frustrations and started scanning the next section of the packet only to be interrupted by the chime of her cell phone. Tempted to ignore it, she changed her mind when the displayed number told her it was Blake. She hadn't seen him since she'd gotten back from New York a few days ago and their phone conversations had been unsatisfying to say the least.

"I need to get this," she told Tessa, who, focused on her paperwork, gave a vague wave in reply.

"Is something wrong?" she asked after their hellos.

"Not that I know of," he said. "Does something need to be wrong for me to call you?"

"Of course not. You just surprised me, that's all."

"Pleasantly, I hope."

"It depends on your reason for calling," she came back lightly and he laughed.

"I wondered if you were doing anything this evening. I thought I might stop by. It's the first chance I've had to see you since you got home."

More than a little curious, she told him, "I don't have any plans. My parents are having dinner with Uncle Peter but I didn't feel up to another fund-raiser disguised as a social event. Is this about the ball?"

"About six, then?" He completely ignored her question. "I'll bring dinner."

"That's fine, but Blake—"

"I'll see you then." And he cut the connection before she could question him any further, leaving her staring at the phone in confusion.

"Wow, it really is true."

Katie looked up to Tessa, her assistant's face avid with interest. "What really is true?" Although she already had a good idea of Tessa's answer.

"You and Blake McCord being an item. He's the last man I would have thought you'd fall for, especially after Tate. I mean he's rich and gorgeous and I'm sure there isn't a lack of women who'd love to get him in bed," Tessa added hastily at Katie's frown. "But I never figured you'd be attracted to the cold, arrogant type."

"You don't know Blake. There's another side to him than the one everyone sees," Katie defended him. "And we're not an item. I like him, we're friends—"

"You're spending tonight with him, apparently just the two of you."

"It's just dinner and talking, and I'm sure it's something to do with the plans for the ball."

"Right," Tessa drawled. "So how long has this been going on? Wait—is he the guy you've been daydreaming about since you and Tate broke up?"

"Tessa—"

"That's the reason you and Tate called your engagement off, because you and Tate's *brother*…?"

"Of course it isn't," Katie said, sounding more defensive than she would have liked. "I told you, Blake and I are friends. We're working on planning the Halloween ball together. That's all there is to it." It was a flat lie, but she couldn't define what she and Blake were beyond that to herself, let alone anyone else. "Even if we were seeing each other, Blake doesn't have anything to do with what happened between Tate and me. Tate and I were over long before then. We just didn't make it official."

"You are seeing Blake, then," Tessa persisted.

Exasperated by Tessa's determination to get her to admit what Katie hadn't decided for herself, she said, "Oh, stop already. Let's just get this paperwork done."

Katie focused on the work in front of her, but Blake and his cryptic call kept distracting her, leaving her wondering, speculating, imagining just what he had in mind for them this evening.

Blake tossed his cell phone on his desk, satisfied he'd successfully convinced Katie to spend an evening with him without the necessity of making an excuse that it had anything to do with the hospital benefit. He wouldn't have resorted to directly lying, but had no qualms about editing what information he did give in order to get his way. If he'd told her his plans for the night, she might have turned him down and he wasn't going to take that chance.

A hesitant tap at his office door interrupted his review of his agenda for the evening and Penny poked her head into the room. "Do you have a minute?"

"What have you got?" Blake asked, gesturing his sister to a chair and accepting the portfolio she handed over the desk.

"These are some of the new designs I've been working on using the canary diamonds. I think you'll like them, at least I hope you will."

"Your work is always good," he told her absently, while looking over the sketches with a critical eye. Perched on the edge of her chair, Penny, her fingers laced tightly together, watched him flip through her efforts. There were a few more modern looking pieces Blake didn't care for, but overall, Penny had used both canary and white diamonds in white gold, silver and platinum settings to give the designs a rich, romantic feeling, as if the jewelry itself was centuries old, yet timeless in its beauty and appeal. He was nearly at the end of the sketches when one ring in particular caught his eye. It was a classic, square cut solitaire set in platinum.

Without taking his eyes off the sketch, he said, "This is something special," and immediately Katie came to mind. He thought she would love this, something unique and beautiful, but not ostentatious, like Katie herself.

"What do you think?" Penny asked and Blake caught the anxious note in her voice.

"That you've done a great job with this, especially these—" He spread out the designs he liked best. "I'm not a big fan of the others, but I suppose it's wise to include them."

"Not necessarily. If you're planning to tie the collection in with the Santa Magdalena diamond, then considering the history behind it, you might want to stick with the more traditional-looking pieces." Looking happier at Blake's praise, Penny started gathering up her sketches. "I like those best, too, so I'll focus more on them."

"Not this." Blake pulled back the sketch of the solitaire ring. "I don't want this included in the collection."

Penny's eyes widened slightly. "I thought you said it was special."

"It is. Which is why I only want one of them."

"*You* want it?"

"Yes, is there a problem?"

"No." Penny dragged out the syllable, eyeing him doubtfully. Blake could see she wanted to pursue the matter, but it wasn't in her nature to push. Instead, she settled for a nod and "All right, if that's what you want." She finished putting her portfolio back together then stood up, readying to leave.

It wasn't the best timing but since he hadn't seen much of Penny lately, and unwilling to let her go before he had his say about a subject that had nothing to do with jewelry designing, he said abruptly, "Are you still seeing Jason Foley?"

Starting, Penny recovered quickly. "I'm not going to talk about that with you." An uncharacteristic defiance settled over her face. "I already know you don't approve. There's no point in us discussing it."

This new show of stubbornness took Blake aback. "Penny—"

"I thought you might understand, at least a little,"

Penny went on, "because of Katie. You should know how it feels when people want to talk about things that are private between two people."

"That's completely different. Katie isn't a Foley."

"It's not different. You just won't see it any other way because of this stupid feud with the Foleys that doesn't mean anything to anyone anymore, except you." With that, Penny turned and almost ran from the room, leaving the door flung open wide behind her and Blake staring at her wake, wondering what the hell had just happened and whether Jason Foley was responsible for this different side of his baby sister.

It was an unwelcome thought. And yet, reluctantly, he could understand how Penny felt having someone dissecting her relationship and telling her it was completely wrong. He wasn't sure where he and Katie stood with each other, but he did resent the attempts by their families, friends and even acquaintances to influence how they felt about each other. He didn't trust Jason Foley; he was sure the only reason Jason was pursuing Penny was because he wanted information about the diamond. On the other hand, maybe his badgering Penny about it was only making things worse by spurring her determination to stick with Jason and prove Blake wrong.

Doubting himself and his certainties made Blake uncomfortable. Katie had more or less accused him of being inflexible and he conceded in some areas, she might be right. When it came to the Foleys, though, he couldn't afford to question himself. Not when he had so much riding on this plan to find the diamond and revive McCord Jewelers.

So for now, he pushed aside his misgivings and

focused his thoughts on the evening ahead and those plans that had more promise of succeeding exactly as he hoped.

Though Blake had made it clear he'd decided the agenda for the evening, Katie determined she'd be the one setting the mood. Blake needed to learn to relax once in a while and she admitted she liked being the one who coaxed him into it. She deliberately dressed casually in jeans and a button-down white shirt, leaving her hair loose, her makeup minimal, and enjoyed his approving look when, promptly at six, she opened the door to him.

"Are you going to tell me what this is about?" she asked, leading him into the kitchen so he could deposit the large hamper he carried. He apparently had been thinking along the same lines as her as far as mood because in khakis and a dark blue shirt, sleeves rolled halfway up his forearms, he looked more dressed down than she'd ever seen him.

"Escape," he answered in a word. "You told me I needed to do it more often."

"And you listened? I didn't know I had that much influence over you." Her lips curved up. "You could be in trouble."

"Be nice. I brought champagne."

"You had an ulterior motive for that."

"And this—" Reaching into the hamper, he handed over a DVD.

It was Bogart's *In A Lonely Place,* one of the few she'd never seen. "If I didn't know better, I'd say you had spies." The smug look on his face stopped her. "How did you—?"

"While you were in New York, I asked your house-keeper to check your collection."

It was so typically Blake, not content to settle for less than perfection in executing a plan, and yet the gesture touched her because he'd cared enough to make the gift and the evening personal to her. "Thank you," she said softly, and pressing her hand to his chest, lightly kissed him. "For all of this. I can't think of a better way to spend the evening."

"Can't you?" His eyes swept over her. "Then I need to try harder."

"I don't think so," she said, quickly shifting the subject from one that evoked dangerously seductive images to one more mundane. Lifting the hamper lid, she peered inside. "What's for dinner?"

"Lasagna and chocolate cheesecake. It seemed like a strange combination but—"

"I know, you talked to the cook, too, and she gave away my secret passions."

Blake laughed. "No, just your favorite dinner."

He helped her unpack the provisions and after a leisurely meal, Katie insisted on carrying the cheesecake and champagne into the den, and having dessert while they watched the movie. She even persuaded Blake to try the combination, giggling at his grimace after one sip. Afterward, it felt natural to sit next to him on the couch, her shoulder brushing his, until eventually, his arm slid around her and she leaned into him.

Katie sighed when the movie ended, stretching as she picked up the remote and switched off the television. "Much better than an evening of politics," she said, sitting back.

"Or business," Blake agreed. He began idly sifting his fingers through her hair, occasionally skimming against her neck, watching the motion as if it fascinated him.

"Blake…" His name came out almost a plea and she wasn't sure if she was reminding him her parents would soon be home and to stop, or asking him to go further than the barest contact he was making on her skin.

He looked up, their eyes met, and later, reliving the moments, Katie could never remember who moved first, only that they were in each other's arms and locked in a kiss that had gone from a tentative caress to sensually explicit so fast it dizzied her. The thought of holding back never crossed her mind. His hands roving her shoulders, her back, made her greedy for every feeling, careless of where they were and who might see them.

Distracted by the openmouthed kisses he dragged along her throat that caused her to arch back, offering him better access, she fumbled blindly with the buttons of his shirt. Finally succeeding in freeing them all, she jerked his shirttails out and spread her hands over his chest, drawing a low groan from him that rumbled against her ear.

She pulled him with her as he eased her down on the couch. Blake claimed her mouth again at the same time he unbuttoned her shirt, pushing it off her shoulders, taking her bra straps with it. The intensity of the sensations felt like a wild slide down a high mountain, an incredible, addictive rush, and so new to her. All those years of being Tate's lover, she'd thought she understood passion. She realized now everything she'd felt before was only a hint of what she could feel, what Blake could make her feel. And she knew Blake shared it from the hungry way he kissed and touched her, as if he'd been holding back for so long and all at once had let go every restraint.

Any inhibitions, any doubts she'd had, burned away.

They'd both lost control of this, if they ever had it to begin with. It was crazy, and exciting, and probably wrong in a hundred ways, but Katie didn't care.

"Don't stop," she murmured in between kissing his neck, along his collarbone.

The sound of her voice seemed to give him pause. "Katie…" Breathing hard, he looked at her and there was something vulnerable in his face, an almost stunned expression. "Are you…is that what you want…here?"

"Yes." She kissed him. "Yes."

His mouth moved hotly against her ear. "Your parents—"

"They're not here."

"But soon…" he muttered at the same time his hand cupped one breast, his caresses becoming more intimate. "I don't want to do this in a hurry."

"Please, Blake." It came out half demand, half begging.

As if he'd come to a decision and it sobered him, Blake straightened, bringing her with him so they faced each other, his hands still gripping her arms. "I want you," he ground out and kissed her hard and fast. "But you deserve better."

For a moment, Katie wasn't sure whether he meant himself or better than a quick tumble on her couch, with the threat of her parents catching them in the act. The thought it could be both quelled her frustration at him stopping and lifted her hand to gently touch his face. "Maybe we both do. But it feels pretty good right now."

"You're not making this easy." Blake groaned, closing his eyes at her touch.

"Sorry," she murmured. She leaned in and pressed her lips to his and he took charge, kissing her slowly, thoroughly, until they were both breathless again, and she was entertaining thoughts of persuading him to throw caution out the window.

Sounds of doors closing, voices and footsteps put an end to that fantasy. They both moved quickly to straighten their clothes and to appear as if the last minutes had never happened. Their attempts, in Katie's eyes, didn't do them much good. Blake's hair was tousled, even more after he ran a hand through it, and he looked ruffled; she doubted she was any better.

"That's probably my cue to leave," he said without much conviction behind it. "They'll have seen my car."

"I guess you should, then. It's late…"

He slid his hand around her nape, pulled her to him, and kissed her, long and deep. "Next time," he promised.

Katie, walking Blake to the door, hoped they could escape her parents notice. She thought she'd gotten lucky when, after a lingering kiss of thanks and goodbye, she saw him off, but her luck ran out almost the moment she turned to retreat to her room.

"It was Blake's car, then," Anna said, coming into the foyer. "I thought you told me you weren't involved beyond the planning for the ball."

"No, you told me we shouldn't be involved," Katie returned. "And as I said before, you're jumping to conclusions."

"Oh, for heaven's sake, Katie, I'm not blind or stupid. It's nearly midnight and you don't kiss a man like that to finalize plans for a ball."

Flushing, Katie stood her ground. "No, but it's time I started making my own choices."

She expected a rebuttal from her mother, repeating all the reasons why Anna thought Blake McCord was wrong for her daughter. Instead, Anna said quietly, "That may be. But are you really sure you know what you want?"

There was no certain answer to that question and for a long time after she left her mother, into the tiny hours of the morning, Katie lay awake, trying to decide if what she wanted from Blake and what she needed were the same thing.

Chapter Nine

Blake found Eleanor in the greenhouse, tending her orchids. It was hard making the trip to his mother's sanctuary in answer to the message she'd left for Blake to find her after work. The last thing he wanted after a day like the one he'd had, having to face the latest reports that McCord's sales were still slipping, was a confrontation with his mother.

But not responding to her would be worse. Then she'd find him, demanding explanations he didn't intend to make.

She looked up from the pot she'd been refilling with the specially mixed fertilizer she used on her prized flowers. "You look tired," she noted, more an idle observation than an expression of sympathy.

Careful not to bump against any of her plants, Blake

stepped a little closer. "I'm fine," he said, brushing her off. "You wanted to see me?"

Eleanor patted the soil with gloved hands then moved the pot she'd been working on from the bench back to its spot on her meticulously kept shelves. She pulled off her gloves and waved Blake to a granite garden bench near her. "Come over and sit down a bit. You've probably been running nonstop all day."

"I have, but frankly, I'd rather relax in the library with a scotch than out here."

"You've never liked my flowers."

Blake rolled his eyes. "That's not true and you know it. I always compliment you on them. I'm just hot in this suit and I'd like to go change and wind down inside."

"I understand, but I wanted to meet with you out here because it's about the only place on this property where two people can have some privacy."

Blake groaned inwardly. He felt a reprimand coming on. And he'd bet the Santa Magdalena Diamond it had everything to do with Katie. "That sounds serious."

"It might be." Eleanor shook out her gardening gloves and placed them neatly beside her little trowel on the workbench. "That's what I want to find out."

"Whatever it is, I'm not sure I can help you. But go ahead."

"I got a call from Anna Salgar." She waited, looking at him as if that said it all.

"And? So what? You two are friends."

"It wasn't about me. It was about you. And Katie."

"Again, my question is, and?"

"I don't appreciate your sarcasm, Blake. You know exactly what I mean."

Blake was not in the mood for what was certain to

soon turn into an all-out interrogation. "Let's be honest. You don't appreciate much about me, Mother."

"That was uncalled for and you know it."

He knew he should have stopped himself but exhaustion, suppressed resentment and a naturally short fuse egged him on. "No, I don't. You've never had any tolerance for my issues, but with Charlie, for example, well, let's face it, he can do no wrong in your eyes."

Eleanor bristled. "I don't see what Charlie has to do with this."

"Nothing, except that if he were seeing a woman you had objections to, you'd still try to find a way to support him."

"This is about you and Katie. It has nothing to do with your brother."

She was partially right and he knew it, but inadvertently she'd opened an old, festering wound in him and this time, maybe for the first time ever, he wasn't going to let her get away without facing it. Katie mattered a great deal to him and he wasn't about to let his mother sabotage what he hoped were the beginnings of something lasting.

"Yes it does, in a roundabout way maybe, but the fact is I know you're going to give me grief about seeing Katie. And, I know if situations were reversed, you would do just the opposite for Charlie. He's half Foley, yet he's always been the golden boy, at least in your eyes."

"He's my youngest," she retorted defensively. "It's typical for mothers to coddle the baby of the family a bit."

"Is it typical that the only time you want to talk to me, it's because you disapprove of something I'm doing?"

Eleanor stood stoically, completely ignoring his accusation. "It's not like you to be petulant."

"I told you, it's been a long day."

"I do appreciate all you do for this family," she told him, softening her tone slightly. "And as for Charlie, this has all been very hard on him. He didn't ask for any of this to happen."

"Neither did I. But then I didn't have much choice, did I?"

Glancing away, Eleanor fidgeted with the leaf of a nearby plant. "Blake, I *am* truly sorry for the terrible stress you're facing now," she said, still avoiding his eyes, until she added, "Don't you think involving yourself with Katie is only adding to that?"

"Look, I don't know what Anna said to you. I probably don't want to know. But for your information and hers, Katie is good for me. She's a beautiful, fun, intelligent woman and I enjoy her company. In fact, unlike most other people, Katie actually helps me relax. She knows how to help me take my mind off business."

"Oh, really?"

"That's not what I meant." Blake balled his fists, struggling to keep his tone from going from sharp to harsh. "I mean she listens and she cares. What the hell is wrong with that?"

"Nothing, of course. If that's all it is. Anna and I are merely concerned about our children's happiness, that's all."

"If that's true, then why don't you both back off and let us live our lives. Neither Katie nor I need you telling us what to do."

"Well, I can see you're not in a mood to listen to me, as usual, so we might as well drop this."

The odd rush of emotion, anger, resentment and frustration from years and years of listening with restraint and respect to his mother's criticisms, corrections, suggestions and demands swelled now in Blake until he thought he would burst into a tirade he knew he would never forgive himself for. Why did her intrusion into his private life feel so much more offensive now than it had ever before?

One word came to mind: Katie.

It was different with her: the way he felt, the need to protect her, them, their privacy, their future. He'd never cared enough about another woman to feel defensive. But now that he and Katie had shifted somehow from friends to whatever they were at present, he wanted nothing more than for his mother, her mother, all of damned Dallas to butt out.

With no small struggle, he banked the worst of his anger and tried to ease out of the conversation and out of Eleanor's space.

"It has nothing to do with my mood. It has more to do with the fact that the only times in my life you've taken a genuine interest in me have been when my decisions might in some way affect or interfere with your life or your plans for my life. By contrast, since Charlie was born, you've always been preoccupied with everything that could possibly help him."

For the first time in as long as he could recall, Eleanor flinched. "That's a horrible thing to say to me."

"I didn't say it to hurt you. I just think it's time for both of us to be honest."

"Well," Eleanor said briskly, now clearly out of her comfort zone, "I promised Anna I'd try to talk to you and so I have. That's all I can do. You've taken this far beyond any conversation *I* intended to have."

"That's the point. If I didn't we'd never have had this

conversation." He turned his back to her. "I'm going to get that scotch now." With that he strode away, leaving his mother to ponder, although he knew she'd never address the issues he raised.

Still, it felt good for once to say what he was really thinking instead of what he knew she wanted to hear. He owed that to Katie, too; she'd given him the motivation.

At that moment he realized he didn't want to have that scotch, or anything else for that matter, without her.

A little concerned but glad to hear from him, Katie wondered at the slightly weary note in Blake's voice when he'd called. It didn't sound at all like him. And asking her to simply take a walk in the park certainly wasn't like him. Nonetheless, she agreed to meet him, wondering what was on his mind.

They found each other at the prescribed spot along the north end of a little known but lushly beautiful park nestled in an unexpected corner of the wealthier Dallas suburbs.

"You're here in time to watch the sun set," Blake said from where he sat stretched comfortably over a wood and wrought-iron park bench, one of several that surrounded a granite fountain and small pool.

"Well, I'd say you look relaxed, except for the pinstripes and tie."

Blake glanced down at his shirt and suit coat. "I forgot to change." He laughed a little at himself. Something few people ever saw him do, Katie mused. "I just needed to get out of that house."

In all the time she'd known him, Katie had never heard him sound quite like this and it worried her. She walked past the spouting water and sat down beside him, instinctively laying a hand on his thigh. "Hey, what's up? You don't seem like yourself at all."

Blake stared off, mesmerized by the rhythm of the fountain's water show. After a long distracted moment he turned to her. Glancing over her, as though part of him just realized she was there, he said, "You look beautiful."

"In sweats and cross-trainers?"

"Especially."

She couldn't help but laugh. "You do surprise me. I was just getting out of the bath when you called—"

"That's not playing fair, Katie, putting that vision in my head."

"Who says I play fair? I threw this on because I didn't actually know what you meant by going for a walk."

"Sorry, I'd love to walk through the park with you, but after I got here and sat down and started watching the sunset I pretty much forgot about the walk."

Now she was truly concerned. Rather than his usual take-control self, he seemed distracted.

"Blake, did something happen today?"

He laughed ruefully. "Your mom called my mom."

She stiffened. "What?"

"If you're up for drama, we could be Romeo and Juliet except for the fact that we're twice their age and ironically *we* aren't the ones from enemy families. Not to say *that* hasn't happened."

Katie knew he was referring to his mother's affair with Rex Foley. Eleanor herself had revealed to Katie a few details of her past with Rex, and both Tate and Gabby had told her about the brief liaison between Eleanor and Rex, the one that produced Charlie. She suspected Blake was also alluding to Penny's new dalliance with Jason Foley.

"Luckily that's not us," she tried to say lightly. When he kept staring off into the pinks and purples lighting the sky above a fading sun, waning remains of what must have been a trying day, she decided to risk being more direct. "Did you and your mother talk about us or about her affair with Rex?"

He shrugged. "Mostly us, but a little of the other. She doesn't like to go there, needless to say." He sat up from his leaning position on the bench, then turned and took her hand in his, running soft patterns over her skin with the pad of his thumb. "She got on my nerves, it's not an issue and it's nothing new. I just needed to get out and away for a while. I needed to be with you."

Katie's heart swelled. That he had thought of her, wanted to be near her when his heart and mind were troubled made her feel more cherished and needed than Tate ever had.

She smiled, leaning into him to touch her lips to his. With a gentle kiss, she murmured, "Thank you."

"For what?"

"Just being here," she said as a substitute for all the things she could have said. "I needed to be with you, too."

They did end up strolling through the park after sunset, holding hands like old lovers by the light of big round gas lamps lighting the tree-canopied trail. In a dozen lifetimes, Blake never would have imagined himself relaxed and actually enjoying a simple walk in the park. Yet surprisingly, he felt more comfortable revealing his feelings to Katie than he had to anyone previously about his mother, her affair with Rex, the uncertain future of McCord Jewelers and his sense of responsibility for that ultimate outcome.

And Katie simply listened. Something no one else in his life had ever done. She didn't offer correction, guilt, advice or make demands. She merely asked a question to clarify here or there, offered a word of encouragement or support and patiently stayed focused on him.

"I'm sorry. I've gone on about my dramas long enough," he said, realizing with a touch of self-consciousness that he'd scarcely asked *her* anything about how things were going in her world.

She turned and smiled up to him. "Don't be sorry, I like it when you talk to me, really talk to me, like you are now."

The soft pools in her eyes told him she meant it. Pausing on the path, he pulled her close. Nuzzling his face in her jasmine-scented hair, he kissed her neck. "Thank you for listening."

"After all these years of knowing each other, I feel like I'm only now getting to know the real you."

"That could be dangerous."

Now averting her eyes to stare out beyond his shoulder, she admitted softly, "It is. But not for the reasons you might think."

"Worried I'm messed up from my mother's fling with Rex Foley and my family's endless expectations?"

"I wouldn't say that." Cupping his chin in her hands, she kissed him slowly, with a tenderness that melted the edges of what felt like an iceberg that had lodged itself somewhere in his heart so long ago he couldn't remember when it hadn't been there.

Blake wrapped his arms around her and matched her kiss, moonlight drenching them in a soft glow. Pliable and willing, she melded to his chest, her supple body inviting him to touch. Sliding his hands down her back, he nudged her closer and when she responded, he deepened their kiss. As it always was between them, it suddenly became urgent—roaming hands, impatient tugging at clothes, forgetting where they were in their need to get even closer.

He could have kept on kissing her but through the moonlit shadows came the approaching sound of giggling teenagers down the path. She drew back and Blake distanced himself reluctantly, both of them resuming their walk.

Trying to catch his breath through a haze of frustrated desire, Blake attempted to attribute the intensity of his need to mere lust. Katie was a stunningly beautiful, sensuous woman after all. But he knew he was lying to himself. What he felt for her went far deeper, down to a place he'd never allowed himself to go.

"That was close," she said finally, with a small laugh, breaking their long silence.

"Do you think they got an eyeful?"

"I doubt it. It's too dark and they weren't that close."

They were nearing the parking lot but he didn't want the night to end here. He had more to say to her, wanted to feel her in his arms again.

She stopped at a fork in the path. "I'm parked over there. It's been so nice, though, just walking and talking. Peaceful, isn't it?"

After pressing her to him until his arousal ached, Blake's body felt anything but peaceful. And his mind wasn't any better. But he lied, lest he scare her off. "We should do this again. It's still early, though. How about a bite to eat?"

"I'd love to but I can't tonight. I left a stack of paperwork for the charity ball unfinished. I'm falling terribly behind and it's getting close."

Her answer hit him hard, like an out-and-out rejection of him personally, not the simple thanks-but-no-thanks he knew it was. His reaction was unreasonable, caused in part he was sure by his unsettling confrontation with his mother, even if it didn't feel like it at the moment. Well trained in stoicism and buried emotions, he simply shrugged it off. "Another time, then."

"Oh, definitely," she said with a light kiss and a squeeze to his hand. "Thank you again for a really lovely evening."

Her gestures and her words left him worse than unsatisfied. The pit of his stomach went hard, felt suddenly cold and empty.

She held the key to a feeling of intimacy he'd never experienced and wasn't sure if he wanted to continue to feel because when she left him, that feeling wrapped itself around his heart like the platinum watch around his wrist, beautiful, essential to the point that without it—without her—he'd begun to feel lost.

Chapter Ten

"Are you sure I can't change your mind?" Blake asked the question, knowing the answer he'd get from Katie, but reluctant to leave without her. They stood together at the gate leading to his private jet, the close warmth of the small room a contrast to the cool gray mistiness of the early fall morning outside the tall glass windows. She'd driven him to the airport today, though it was unnecessary, but her presence wasn't enough to dispel his doubts about yet another separation. Since he'd made plans, two days ago, to make a quick trip to Toronto to personally complete the purchase of several canary diamonds, he'd been plagued by the uneasy feeling that he was going to regret walking away from Katie at this juncture of their relationship, even briefly. If he could call what they had a relationship in terms of it being more than friendship or simple desire, and that was something he hadn't allowed himself to consider too closely yet.

She shook her head, her small smile regretful. "You know I can't. Between work and finalizing the plans for the ball…I wish I could, though."

"Do you?" He stopped her from answering, lightly shaping her cheek with his fingertips. "Katie—" This time he hesitated, uncertain of what he wanted to say to her, more unsure of his own feelings.

"It's only for two days," she said. "We'll both be busy. And you'll be back by the weekend."

"Who are you trying to convince that this doesn't matter?"

"Both of us, I guess. Is it working?"

"Not at this end," Blake told her flatly.

A faint color stained her cheeks. "Why was this not an issue when I went to New York?"

"Hell if I know. Maybe because things haven't been quite the same since you came back."

"I'm not sure what *the same*—" she gave a slight emphasis to the words "—is with us. Are you?"

"No, but I'd like the chance to define it. I'd like to think that you do, too."

Her hesitation was damning, adding to his overall uneasiness that something had changed between them and not for the better. "I'll take that as a no," he said shortly.

"It's not that." She briefly bit her lower lip before reaching out to smooth her hand over his shoulder, following the gesture with her eyes. "If I could just think clearly around you…"

"The feeling's mutual." And before she could protest, Blake pulled her into his arms and lowered his mouth to hers. Neither of them seemed capable of doing anything by half measure and their kiss deepened while she put her arms around his neck and pressed herself closer.

After what seemed to him too short a time, she eased away, pushing both hands through her hair. "This is what I'm talking about. How can we decide what we want and need from each other, or if there's even an *us* to begin with, if we end every discussion like this?"

"It's not every discussion."

"Blake—"

"What do you want from me, Katie?" he asked, beginning to get frustrated, although he knew his irritation stemmed more from his own unsettled feelings than her questions.

"I could ask you the same thing," she countered.

It was on the tip of his tongue to give a glib answer, the one she probably expected: that he wanted her in his bed, no strings attached, no hearts broken. Except this time, with her, the words he'd said to women so many times before in so many different ways didn't come easily—or at all.

"I don't think either of us has an answer right now," Katie said quietly. "This should wait. We can talk when you get back from Toronto."

Blake wanted to argue but time was short and rationally he knew they couldn't resolve anything here and at this moment. The problem was he didn't feel very rational. He forced a deep breath, reined in his urge to blow off the trip entirely, and kissed her cheek, the chaste caress of a friend.

"I'll call you this evening," he said, "if it's not too late."

She responded with a nod and with what might have been an attempt at a smile and stepped back to let him leave.

Taking that as his dismissal, he turned, intending to board the jet, but barely completed the motion before he spun back around, strode over to her and gave her the kiss he wanted, nothing chaste about it. He didn't wait for her response; instead he headed in the opposite direction, refusing to look back.

It was the next morning when her cell phone rang and Katie, automatically assuming it was Blake calling her to confirm she'd be picking him up tomorrow afternoon, frowned a little when she realized it wasn't him, but a number she didn't recognize.

"Katie, this is Marcus Brent." A voice answered her hello and Katie recognized it as her Uncle Peter's campaign manager.

"Marcus, hello. This is a surprise." No lie there; she scarcely knew him, except from their encounters at various fund-raisers. He was in his midforties, successful and good looking in a sleek, polished way. She'd thought little about him except as a key player in her uncle's campaign and had never had more than a superficial conversation with him, which made her wonder why he was calling her now. "If this is about another fund-raiser, fair warning—I've had my fill."

Marcus laughed. "No, this is personal. If you're free this evening, I wanted to ask if you'd have dinner with me. I realize it's short notice," he went on when, caught off guard, she didn't answer right away, "but this close to the election, my schedule is pretty tight. Everything I do these days seems like last minute."

A vision of Blake crossed her mind, clashing with remembered advice from family and friends that she shouldn't limit herself to one man, and her own uncertainties over her involvement with Blake so soon after Tate.

What do you want from me, Katie? She heard Blake's voice in her mind. Instead of answering him, she'd hedged, throwing the question back at him because she didn't know what to say. That was the problem and it prompted her to impulsively tell Marcus, "Thank you, I'd like that. What time?"

It was only after they'd settled the details and she hung up, that she was hit by a mass of regrets and the feeling she'd just made a mistake she wouldn't soon rectify.

The feeling stayed with her even as she tried to reason with herself that she was doing the sensible thing, not limiting herself to the first man she'd been strongly attracted to, considering for once what she really wanted in a relationship. In a way, she and Blake shared a lack of experience in sustaining anything more long-term or in-depth than a passionate affair, and while it was tempting, she knew it wouldn't satisfy her need for something loving and lasting.

Her private pep talk carried her through the evening's dinner with Marcus and although the date wasn't a disaster, she ended it early, pleading a first-thing-in-the-morning appointment, vague about when she'd be able to see him again. He lightly kissed her good-night and she silently thanked him for not pressing it further because all she felt was a sense of guilt that she carried with her to the airport the next afternoon.

Comparisons immediately came to mind when Blake strode over to where she waited and skipped a hello in favor of a long kiss, except there was really no comparison. She forgot Marcus had ever touched her the moment Blake's mouth covered hers and her nagging conscience caused her to kiss Blake back all the more passionately.

"If that's what I have to look forward to every time I leave town, then I'll have to do it more often," he said, holding her a little away from him.

"I missed you, that's all."

"Did you?"

"Why is that so hard to believe?"

"I don't know." She averted her eyes from his searching look. "Did something happen while I was gone?"

"A lot of things happened," she quipped back, "but none of them were important. Just the usual. Are you ready to go? And am I taking you home or to your office?"

Blake hesitated, watching her a few moments longer, and then picked up the locked case and suit bag he'd set down at his feet before he'd scooped her into his arms. "Home is fine. I can stow these—" he indicated the case she assumed held the diamonds "—in the safe there for the time being."

They were out of the airport and a few minutes on the road when he broke the silence, causing her to start. "Is everything all right?"

"Of course, yes. Everything is fine."

"Are you sure? You seem very tense."

The note of concern that warmed his voice nearly caused her to blurt out her jumbled thoughts. *I cheated on you. That's the way it feels. Except it can't be cheating when we haven't promised each other anything, and it's ridiculous to think of having dinner with another man as a betrayal.* "I have a lot of things on my mind right now," she said and it wasn't wholly a lie. "Work has been busy and the ball is coming up fast..."

"Is that all?" Blake persisted.

"Isn't that enough?" She didn't dare glance his way.

"I suppose it is." He fell quiet again and they were less than five minutes from the McCord estate before he spoke up again. "Will you have dinner with me tonight? There's a new French restaurant on the west side—"

"No." Blake raised a brow at her sharp protest and she quickly amended, "I mean yes, I'll have dinner with you, but not French. I'd rather do something more casual." Marcus had taken her to an expensive French restaurant and the last thing she wanted was to be reminded of it the entire evening with Blake.

"I'd invite you home, but—" His mouth pulled in a wry grimace.

"But that would be weird," she agreed. "Under the circumstances, I don't think I'm quite ready for an intimate family dinner." She'd reached the mansion and pulled into the long drive, stopping near the front. After a moment, she shifted to face him.

Expecting him to reach for her, she was surprised and admittedly disappointed when he didn't make good on the clear desire she saw in his face. "How about an intimate night with me?"

The soft, low timbre of his voice sent a shiver through her. "Are we still talking about dinner?"

"I don't know, are we?" Blake asked and the caress of his eyes on her was nearly as potent as a physical touch.

"I thought we were going to talk," she said, aggravated it came out slightly breathless, giving away her own desires.

"Who said that?"

"We did, before you left town."

"That was you."

"Blake—"

"Okay," he said, holding up a hand. "We'll talk. I'll pick you up at six." He let himself out of the car, retrieved his bags and then leaned back inside and before he let her leave added with that cocksure half smile curling one side of his mouth, "Remember, though— you didn't define the topic."

Blake had accepted Katie's earlier mood, taking her word it was the pressures of work and the upcoming benefit that were responsible for her odd edginess. He wondered, though, as he pulled into the drive of the Salgar estate precisely at six, if her insistence they "talk" had more to do with defining their relationship than work and party plans. She'd seemed happy enough to see him, as willing as he to pick up where they'd left off. But it was also clear something had changed, that she wanted more from him than he'd ever been asked to give.

Knowing that forced him to consider the question she'd thrown back at him and he'd never answered, what did *he* want from her? The answer had become increasingly complex, extending beyond desire, to friendship, caring, warmth—things he'd learned to live without but had come to rely on from Katie.

Halfway through dinner he was still thinking about it, unaware of being lost in his thoughts until Katie's slim fingers brushed his hand.

"Is it jet lag or me?" she asked, the slight curve of her lips making it a tease.

"Neither. I'm sorry, I let myself get distracted thinking of all the things I need to catch up on."

Katie pulled a face. "You're supposed to be relaxing, forgetting all of that until tomorrow."

"I could say the same about you," he returned. He

took her hand, rubbing patterns against her skin with the pad of his thumb. "What's wrong, Katie? Are you having second thoughts about us?"

"Is there an us?" she asked pointedly.

"Do you want there to be?"

"That isn't an answer." She sighed, fiddled with the edge of her napkin. "I want to say yes, but I'm not sure if that's wise."

Blake leaned back in his chair, letting his hand slide from hers. "Because of Tate?"

"Tate?" Her eyes jerked to his and Blake swore he saw guilt flash in her eyes. "No, Tate has nothing to do with this." Her firm denial was at odds with her uncertain expression.

"Then what does—or should I be asking who?"

"If there's a 'who,' it's me. I've never thought about what I want in a relationship and I don't think you have, either. I feel like we've rushed into this blindly just because we're…attracted."

"Attracted?" he repeated with a lifted brow. "I don't think it's anything that tame."

A flush stained her cheeks. "No, and like I said before, it's just complicating things." She took a deep breath, slowly let it go and then squarely met his gaze. "You asked me what I wanted from you. I'm not sure, yet, but I'm worried that whatever it is will be more than you're willing to give me."

She was being honest with him and he owed her the same in return. "I can't make you any promises because you're right, I don't know any more than you how to make this work long-term. I can only say I'm willing to try, if you are."

Looking at him a long moment, Katie surprised him

by leaning over and kissing him. "You must be serious," she said softly, "because I'm pretty sure that's the first time I've heard you admit there's something you don't know how to do."

"Don't let it get around. My reputation will be ruined."

They shared a smile and the mood lightened, lingered the remainder of the evening. It was only much later, when he'd left her at her front door after reluctantly ending their passionate embrace, that he realized that she hadn't answered in kind his offer to work toward a commitment.

Chapter Eleven

Why on earth had she agreed to this?

Seven o'clock on a Saturday, and instead of buried under blankets, taking advantage of the chance to sleep in, she was on the court at the Westwood Tennis Club about to play a mixed doubles match against her ex-fiancé and his new love.

Stretching her back and legs out at the net, she turned to Blake where he stood on the sideline, fiddling with his racquet, pacing, looking anything but relaxed. "Remind me again why I went along with this idea of yours."

"You were the one who decided it would be a good way to quiet the gossips if we were seen socializing with Tate and Tanya," he said shortly. "My only contribution was suggesting tennis."

"I thought we'd both decided." When he only shrugged, his mouth pulled in a hard line, Katie felt a twinge of uneasiness. "If you didn't want to do this, I wish you'd have said something."

"It seemed important to you so I went along with it."

Ready to push him to elaborate on that, Katie was interrupted by the arrival of their opponents.

"Morning all." Tate and Tanya, racquets in hand, waltzed lightly onto the court. Tanya looked fresh and glowing, Tate as handsome as ever.

The foursome exchanged somewhat strained greetings and Blake immediately took control. "We'd better get started, we're running late."

"I have to warn all of you, I haven't played in months," Katie said as they moved onto the court, "and I wasn't that great to begin with."

"Always the modest one," Tate teased, drawing a questioning look from his partner.

When the serve was decided and Blake set the ball in motion, Katie saw the spirit of competition flare in Tanya's eyes. A trait that came in handy in her career as an investigative reporter, no doubt. Inwardly Katie groaned. She'd never been much of a competitor in sports and now playing against her ex and his girlfriend, she felt even more uncomfortable.

"Nice work," Blake praised her when she, surprising herself, caught a ball at the net and killed it before Tanya had a prayer of returning it.

With a graciousness that may have been slightly forced, Tanya echoed the compliment. "If that was any indication of how she plays when she's rusty, we're in trouble, Tate."

Tate shrugged lightly. "Told you."

They volley bantered on at a clipped pace, and Katie began to relax as she realized Tate and Tanya, while strong competitors, were truly making an effort to be supportive and keep the atmosphere as tension-free as possible.

Game after game, she and Blake began to learn more about each other's styles, strengths and weaknesses. She found herself relaxing, working with him as a teammate, enjoying their wins, accepting their losses.

"Match," Tate called out on the final shot. "Looks like we're pretty well tied. Want to call it a day?"

Blake wiped the sweat from his brow, a simple motion that sent Katie's mind to flights of fancy. She found him even sexier with his hair mussed, the muscles in his arms and legs pulsing with power, glistening with sweat.

Tanya caught her staring and smiled a woman-to-woman kind of appreciation. She walked to the net to congratulate Katie on the game and took her hand warmly. "Nice view, hmm?"

Katie couldn't help but smile. "It seems to run in the family."

Tate and Blake shook hands, as well, and Blake put an arm around Katie's waist, lightly holding her to his side. For a moment, it felt awkward, the display of familiarity in front of his brother, but it passed when she saw Tate smile.

"Drinks on me," Blake offered. "Do you two have time for the juice bar?"

Tate turned to Tanya. "I think so, don't you? We aren't due to meet up with Charlie for a couple of hours."

Tanya nodded. "Juice sounds great."

"You have plans with Charlie?" Blake asked sharply.

Tate and Tanya exchanged a glance. "He asked if we could catch up with him for a late lunch."

"I didn't know you and Charlie palled around much."

The edge in Blake's voice was telling. Katie knew

that ever since Eleanor revealed Charlie was actually Rex Foley's son, Blake's relationship with his youngest brother had been strained.

"We don't. He's too busy at the university and with my surgery schedule we hardly ever get to see each other. But…"

"What's going on?"

Katie saw Tanya slide her hand into Tate's. "Honestly, I don't know. All he said was he wanted to talk to me." He stopped, considering, then went on. "He said it has to do with Mom and Rex."

"I see," Blake said flatly. "Well, good luck with that, then." He turned and gestured to Katie. "How about that juice?"

Tension electric between them, the foursome headed toward the front of the club.

The poshly appointed juice bar featured every fruit, basic to exotic, and dozens of add-ons to boost energy, relieve stress or curb hunger. All around them, people sipped icy concoctions in tall, brightly colored glass goblets.

As Katie perused the menu, having skipped break-fast—her stomach beginning to growl—she failed to see the man stride up beside her. She was the last at her table to realize he was trying to get her attention.

Marcus Brent touched her shoulder lightly, breaking her concentration. Her eyes darted upward; her stomach plummeted. She felt all eyes on her and was certain her face had turned a dozen shades of red.

"I didn't realize you were a member here," Marcus said smoothly, turning to the rest of the group. "Hello, Blake," he said, extending a hand. When Blake's eyes looked questioningly at him, he added, "We met at Peter

Salgar's fund-raiser. I'm his campaign manager. It was a pleasant surprise to see you there." He paused. "And to see you here, Katie."

Katie saw Blake struggle to make sense of Marcus's familiarity with Katie. "Right, sorry, it took me a moment to place you," he said finally, taking Marcus's hand.

Marcus turned to Tate and Tanya. "And you must be Tate McCord and the lovely Tanya Kimbrough. I used to see you on the news, now I see your picture in the society column. Neither of them does you justice."

No stranger to compliments, Tanya thanked Marcus graciously. "You did a superb job on the recent campaign ads for Peter. Brilliant, really."

"Thanks, but it was a team effort."

Blake pulled out an empty chair beside him. "Have a seat. We were just getting some refreshments after the game."

Marcus shot Katie an amused glance.

He's enjoying this! she seethed inwardly, wishing she could disappear.

"I'd love to." Marcus took the seat. "But I'll only stay a minute. I don't want to interrupt and I have a game in ten."

"So, have you known the Salgars long?" Blake asked, glancing at Katie.

It was all she could do not to visibly squirm. Instead she focused intently on her mango-raspberry smoothie.

"Not really. Peter hired me after noticing some work I'd done managing campaigns in San Diego and Austin. He made me an offer I couldn't refuse, so I moved here."

"And after this campaign?" Tate asked.

"Well," Marcus said with a little laugh, "I guess that depends on how it turns out." Focusing on Katie, he added, "But I have become quite fond of the Salgars, so it would be difficult to move again."

Reluctantly, Katie pried her eyes from her nearly empty glass. "Oh, yes, Uncle Peter and my parents speak highly of you. I'm sure Uncle Peter would give you an excellent reference—whichever way the campaign goes."

"None of that talk," Marcus teased. "There's only one way for this campaign to end, with a win. But enough about politics. From what I hear, McCord Jewelers is a much more fascinating topic *du jour*."

"I doubt that," Blake said. There was a warning note in his voice that Marcus either didn't recognize or chose to ignore.

"I read in the business journal recently that a couple of stores were closed. I hope everything is okay."

"Reorganization. It has to be done from time to time to cut the fat and raise efficiency. It's routine."

Marcus checked his watch and shoved back in his chair. Standing, he again reached for Blake's hand, then Tate's. "Glad to hear that's all it is. Even long-standing empires hit hard times now and then." Smiling broadly, he offered Tanya a nod and again, touched a hand to Katie's shoulder. "You'll ring me sometime, won't you? We can do dinner again. Maybe Italian next time."

If he hadn't turned and strode briskly away, Katie would have been tempted to dump her smoothie down the front of his sparkling white tennis shirt.

Tanya, bless her feminine compassion, tugged at Tate's arm. Katie avoided both brothers' glares and smiled at Tanya. "If we don't leave now we're going to be late to meet Charlie. And I'm not stepping out into public with this hair and these drenched clothes I've been soaking in too long already."

Taking the not-too-subtle prodding, Tate laid a hand on Blake's back. "Thanks for the game. We'll have to do it again sometime."

Blake nodded absently, his face locked in a hard, stoic frown. "Say hello to Charlie," he ground out.

Katie knew his tone was due in part at least to Marcus's untimely appearance. When Tate and Tanya had left, she had no option but to face him. But what could she say? How could she defend herself for something so minor and meaningless to her, yet so magnified now that it looked like a calculated deception to Blake. Again, murderous thoughts toward Marcus crossed her mind.

"Blake, about Marcus—"

Blake stood, held up a palm. "Save it. I'll go have your car brought around."

At the tense set of his face, a wave of guilt washed over her. And then defensiveness took over. She hadn't done anything wrong. They weren't officially a couple and she *was* officially single and could do as she pleased. Hadn't she convinced herself she needed to give herself time to discover what she really wanted in a relationship?

Or so she'd told herself. The idea she had hurt him, though, quelled some of her rebelliousness. He was the one who'd offered to work toward something long-term; she was the one who'd hesitated and then decided to test the dating waters with Marcus.

"It was only one dinner, when you were in Toronto," she said finally.

"I don't want the details, thanks."

"I don't have that many to give. It's not as if we were lovers. I spent a few hours with him, that's all."

"You're free to see whomever you like." He echoed her own thoughts, but hearing them spoken aloud in his cold, expressionless tone renewed with a vengeance all her uncomfortable feelings. "I need to go. I have to stop by my office. I'll mention your car on my way out."

"Blake—" Katie put a hand on his arm, stopping him from turning to leave. "Can we at least talk about this?"

"What is there to talk about? You decided to date someone else. End of story."

"No, it's not. You're obviously upset about it."

"I don't think my reaction matters one way or the other. You didn't consider it when you chose to go out with Marcus Brent." They locked gazes for brief seconds and then Blake blew out a breath, shoving a hand through his hair. "This is pointless."

"I don't want to leave things like this," Katie said, at a loss to know how to fix it.

"What do you want, Katie? My blessing on your decision to play the field? Sorry—" He pulled free of her grasp. "I can't do that. But you don't need my approval. As you keep pointing out, we're just *friends*."

Not giving her time to respond, he spun around and strode out of the bar, leaving her alone with her regrets.

A last-minute invitation to a fashion show that afternoon in downtown Dallas was unwelcome to say the least. But it was Gabby who'd called to invite her and as they'd been trying for weeks to do lunch or a drink, Katie couldn't possibly say no, even though the invitation included Anna and Eleanor. Still, after the confrontation with Blake, the last thing Katie wanted was to be gently but expertly interrogated by her mother, Eleanor and Gabby.

As they took their seats front row to the catwalk, Katie wished she'd made an excuse to stay home.

"I can't wait to see a sneak preview of the spring Milan collection," Gabby was saying excitedly. "We're so lucky to have gotten in today. It's a small, private showing, but my friend is the designer's cousin. I owe her big-time." She focused on Katie and her grin turned to a small frown. "Are you all right? I know this was last minute. Did I interrupt something?"

"No, it's not that." Realizing she probably looked as if she were sulking, Katie made an effort to brighten her tone. "I'm a little tired, that's all. We played several games of mixed doubles at the club this morning. I haven't played that much tennis in months."

"We? Meaning you and Blake?"

"Against Tanya and Tate," she said, nodding.

At the sound of her sons' names, Eleanor craned her head around to join the conversation. "Did I hear Blake and Tate mentioned in the same breath?"

Katie's stomach tightened, afraid Eleanor would use the moment to quiz her about Blake. "Yes, we all played tennis together this morning."

"Oh…well, that must have been interesting."

"It was fun, actually."

"Look, ladies, the show is starting." Anna pointed to the head of the stage where a glamorous woman with a microphone had appeared from behind the curtains. "That's Margo Hererra. You know her, she's the new designer from Spain."

Gabby smiled. "I told you this would be worth changing your Saturday afternoon plans."

Katie didn't know her or care, but she smiled obligingly.

As all heads turned, riveted toward the stage, the

noise and excitement allowed Katie a welcome respite from conversation. Though appearing to pay attention to the glittering swirl around her, she was in fact miles away. She wished she'd tried harder to convince Blake to talk to her. She hated how they'd left things and wondered if she'd broken whatever bond existed between them.

After a span of time Katie couldn't have recalled, Eleanor leaned toward her. "It's almost over and it's cocktail hour so what do you say the four of us steal away early and grab an appetizer and a martini?"

They shared Anna's Mercedes sedan to a trendy little restaurant nearby and took a corner table near the window where they could people watch and comment on Dallas fashion—or the lack thereof.

"You seem under the weather today, Katie," Eleanor was saying as the waitress handed them their drinks. "Too much tennis?"

"No, not at all. Tanya is a lot of fun and she and Tate are so good together. I'm happy for them."

"What about Tate?" Anna asked.

"What do you mean?"

"Well," she said, stirring the olive around the bottom of her glass with her finger, "it must be difficult for him to see you and Blake dating."

"Why? He's engaged to be married. And anyway Blake and I aren't—" Katie stopped midsentence when all eyes stared her down, letting her know they weren't buying it. "Okay, so we've been seeing each other, but—"

"But what?" Gabby asked, her voice gentle.

Katie hesitated, then, figuring Marcus wouldn't keep it a secret, said, "I don't know how much Blake and I are going to be seeing each other from now on. He found out that I had a date with Marcus Brent while he was in Toronto."

"Oh, Katie, that's wonderful," Anna said, reaching over to pat her daughter's hand. At Katie's disbelieving look, she added hastily, "I didn't mean that quite the way it sounded. It's just dating more than one person is the healthy thing to do, don't you agree?" she asked, directing the question to Eleanor.

"Absolutely. You and Tate were together so long, Katie. You shouldn't limit yourself to one man too quickly."

Gabby listened in silence and Katie felt her friend's empathy. Finally, Gabby politely interrupted the twosome. "Excuse me, but none of us has asked Katie if *she's* glad she dated someone else. Are you?"

Katie's first instinct was to say that it was a horrible mistake and she was worried Blake wouldn't forgive her. Instead she banked that flood of emotions and turned the tables on Gabby. "Did you date anyone else after you and Rafael were involved?"

"I barely looked at another man after Rafael. I was smitten, as they say." She lifted a brow and grinned, catlike. "Not that I let him know that."

Is that the way I feel with Blake? It seemed an almost tame description of the volatile mix of desire, need and communion she felt when they were together.

She turned to Eleanor and Anna. "What about you? Is that the way you felt?" As soon as the words fell from her lips she wished she could have swept them up and away. Of course Eleanor had been head over heels—but for Rex Foley, not Devon McCord.

Anna answered first, rescuing her friend. "In a manner of speaking, yes, I fell for your father the first time I saw him. But it took time to truly fall in love with him."

"I'd be lying if I said Devon and I were ever really in love with each other, even after so many years together," Eleanor said quietly, after a long silence. "All of you know that isn't true. But Rex—I think I fell in love with Rex the first time I saw him. To this day, the thought of him can bring back those feelings. And now, the problem is Blake and the other children know it. Blake, in particular, resents me."

Katie didn't know what to say to comfort her. It was true. Blake had a rigid, hard side she doubted anyone would ever penetrate. "I think he's working on accepting it," she managed, "but with Charlie as a reminder, it's, well, it's going to take time."

"I hope that's all it will take," Eleanor said sadly. "Blake is so angry at me and it's caused a rift between him and Charlie."

Gabby reached out to take Eleanor's hand. "It's a shock, that's all. They're brothers. They'll work it out eventually."

"I hope that's true. But enough about my dramas," Eleanor said, pasting a smile back on her face. "What we want to know is, how was your date?"

Back in the hot seat, Katie sighed. She was with friends; she might as well tell them the truth. "It was fine."

"But?" Anna prompted.

"But he wasn't Blake."

Gabby's smile comforted her. "That says a lot."

"Maybe, but it probably doesn't matter now. We ran into Marcus at the club and he made a point of letting Blake know we had dinner together. Blake didn't take it well." Inwardly, Katie winced at the definite understatement.

"Oh." Eleanor waved a hand. "His ego is just bruised. You know how proud my son is. He'll get past it. And my guess is when he does, now that he knows he has competition, he'll pursue you even harder just to prove he's the better man."

With that all four women lifted their glasses and toasted what they'd managed to turn from Katie's disaster into Katie's accidental victory.

As she took a sip of her drink, Katie wished she could believe Eleanor was right, but the wounded rage in Blake's eyes when he'd left her made it hard to hold on to the hope it was true.

Chapter Twelve

Two pages left to go and Blake was starting to question how he and Katie had managed to get through the past hour's worth of last-minute checklists for the ball without saying more than a few sentences to each other. On the other hand, the strained silence between them spoke volumes.

They hadn't really talked, except impersonally about business or the benefit, since he'd found out about her date with Marcus. Because of that he'd been surprised when she'd agreed to meet him this evening at his office to go over the final list of donations for the silent auction. He hated the distance separating them. It seemed vast, despite them sitting side by side on his office couch, paperwork spread over the coffee table. But he didn't know how to deal with his jealousy or the idea he couldn't dislodge that she didn't place much value on their relationship or consider it serious to begin with. It would be easier if he could simply dismiss his feelings and move on, but he hadn't been able to command his emotions as easily as he did everything else in his life.

"I don't think we've actually gotten this painting yet," Katie said, frowning at a notation on one of their lists. She leaned over to pick up another paper at the same time Blake reached for the same one and their hands touched.

The inadvertent contact froze them midmotion. Their eyes met and Blake saw in hers the same desire that had been tormenting him.

"Blake…" The way she said his name, with both longing and uncertainty, snapped his restraint.

All the pent-up tensions of the past days loosened at once. He pulled her against him and she met him halfway, kissing him back with an intensity that overwhelmed his every other thought and feeling except wanting her closer. Taking control away from him, she pushed gently at his shoulders to urge him back against the couch and they ended up with her half lying on his chest.

He took advantage of the position to slide his hands under her thin sweater and over warm, smooth skin, emboldened by the hum of pleasure she made to drag the material higher, giving him access to rove over her back and the sides of her breasts. Her body and hands rubbing, caressing him, nearly drove him to forget patience and propriety, strip off her clothes and his, and take and give what they both wanted.

It struck him this might be all he would ever have with her. She hesitated when they came too close to deepening their relationship, but she never hesitated in this. And if this was all he could have, maybe he could pretend it would be enough.

"Let's get out of here," he murmured, nuzzling her neck.

Her fingers found their way inside his shirt and teased open the first few buttons. "Where?"

"Anywhere with a bed and no chance of being interrupted." Blake paused his explorations long enough to shift to look at her. "We can take the jet, go somewhere for the weekend and finish this in private."

"Finish this?" she echoed and a wary note crept into her voice. "This, being together—or us?"

Blake sat up, bringing her with him, although he didn't fully let her go. "There isn't really an 'us,' is there? You obviously aren't committed to me in any way."

"And you're committed to me?"

"I'm not the one who decided to see other people the minute you left town."

"It was one date! I needed to—"

"Figure out what you want, so you've told me. But you said yourself our wanting each other was getting in the way, making things more complicated. If we spend a couple of days together we can satisfy it and go back to the way things were before."

"Let me get this straight," she said slowly. "You think a few days of casual sex will fix everything."

The honest answer was he didn't. But he also didn't believe she wanted anything else. "You can't tell me it isn't what you want, too."

For a moment, she stared at him in stunned silence. He waited, expecting her to tell him he was right, that sexual chemistry was all they had and would ever have, and that a weekend in bed would cure them both of the lust that was interfering with their friendship.

Instead, she suddenly jerked out of his hold and to her feet, swinging around to look him squarely in the eye. "No."

"No?" The word caught him off guard. He stood up, halting his step toward her when she thrust out a hand. "Katie—"

"No, Blake. I'm sure you're not used to hearing it, but the answer's no." She pressed a hand to her face for a moment, briefly shutting her eyes, and Blake noticed her trembling, as if she were on the verge of tears.

Only then did he realize he'd made a huge mistake.

"I can't believe, after everything that's happened, that you can be so—" she struggled over the words "—cold."

Blake shoved both hands through his hair, fighting the urge to grab her back into his arms and speak to her with his body, the only way they managed to communicate clearly, it seemed. "What am I supposed to think, Katie? You keep telling me you don't know what you want. But every time I touch you—"

A sharp rap at the office door cut off Blake's sentence. He considered ignoring it or telling whoever it was to leave them the hell alone, but when he looked at Katie to see if she shared his feeling, she made a helpless gesture and turned away.

Cursing under his breath, Blake strode over and yanked open the door, surprised to find Charlie standing there. Hands jammed in the pockets of his jeans, shifting from foot to foot, his younger brother appeared uneasy about his reasons for showing up at Blake's door.

"What are you doing here?" Blake snapped out, letting his frustration speak before he could temper his greeting. "You're supposed to be at school. Did something happen?"

"No, or at least not anything you're thinking. I need to talk to you alone. It's important," Charlie persisted when Blake showed no sign of giving way.

Blake nearly refused, except the determination on Charlie's face told him his brother wasn't going to accept being dismissed before he'd had his say. Blowing out an irritated breath, Blake moved back from the doorway. "Come in, then. Whatever it is, you can say it in front of Katie," he added at Charlie's hesitation at seeing Katie standing there.

"I should go," Katie started, not wanting to be another source of friction between the two brothers. "I need to—"

"Stay," Blake cut her off. "We don't have any secrets from you."

Their gazes locked and after a brief silent battle of wills, she nodded, and sat back down on the couch, her stiff posture telegraphing her awkwardness with the situation.

Shaking his head at the chair Blake offered him, Charlie remained standing, facing Blake, his tension over whatever he'd come to say radiating of him. It gave Blake the unwelcome feeling that whatever his brother had come to tell him, he wasn't going to like it.

"I'm going to meet with my father tomorrow."

Charlie broke the news without any preliminaries and for a few long moments, there was a taut silence, with him and Blake staring at each other like adversaries about to do battle.

Katie fervently wished she'd defied Blake and left when she had the chance. No matter what Blake said, she didn't belong here, witnessing what should have been a very private conversation. She looked between the brothers, knowing from the hardened set of Blake's face he wasn't going to take Charlie's blunt announcement well.

Shifting her glance to Charlie, she recognized the same unshakeable resolve she'd seen so many times in Blake; she also, with new eyes, saw how much he resembled his father. Although he shared Blake and Tate's lean build, he had the dark good looks of the Foley men, and she questioned why no one, herself included, had ever noticed how Charlie McCord stood out like a changeling amongst his own family.

It was Blake who finally ended the quiet. "I assume you're talking about Rex Foley," he said tightly. His hands flexed at his sides. "How can you be sure he wants to meet you, or that he even knows you're his son?"

"He knows," Charlie said. "Mom told him."

The revelation took Katie aback. She wondered if Eleanor had thought about how much angst she'd be causing both families by revealing a twenty-one-year-old truth. If Eleanor had believed it would somehow reconcile the two families, then she had far underestimated how deeply the antipathies between the Foleys and McCords ran.

"She told him," Blake repeated. He shook his head sharply in disbelief. "I don't know why I'm surprised."

"She should have told him—and me—a long time ago."

"She should have stayed away from Rex Foley."

The harsh condemnation breached Charlie's outward calm, leaving him scowling. "And maybe you should have stayed away from Tate's girl, but it doesn't seem to have stopped you."

The cold, unforgiving anger taking control of

Blake's features prompted Katie to her feet and she moved to his side. Underneath the tempering hand she curled over his forearm she could feel the steely clench of muscle.

"I'm not the one who slept with the enemy," Blake ground out. "And you've apparently decided to join them."

"I'm a Foley, whether you like it or not," Charlie countered, not backing down from Blake's fury. "You can't change what happened. Everyone's just going to have to find a way to live with it."

"What do you hope to gain by all this?"

"It's not a matter of gain. I want to know my father. Why can't you understand that?" Pacing a few steps back and forth, Charlie swung on his brother again. "I'm not who I thought I was, all these years. I need to do this."

"So as usual you get whatever you want and damn the consequences to anyone else, is that right?"

Katie gave credit to Charlie for keeping a hold on his own temper, though he looked like he wanted to take a swing at Blake. "I didn't ask for this."

"You don't seem too devastated by it, either," Blake shot back. "Why did you bother coming to tell me? You can't seriously believe I'd approve."

"No, but I thought you might understand. Obviously, I was wrong." Not waiting for Blake's reply, Charlie spun around and strode out the door, leaving it hanging open.

"Son of a—" Turning away from Katie, Blake slammed a fist onto his desktop, rattling everything on it.

Cautious about approaching him in this mood, his angry display unsettled her further. Katie, though, couldn't completely back away from him. "I'm sorry," she said quietly. "This must be hard, especially with everything else going on—"

"What the hell does he think he's doing? He knows how I—most of the family—feel about the Foleys."

"He wants to know his father." She stood up to the glare he fixed on her. "He's right, what happened between your mother and Rex isn't his fault. You can't blame Charlie for trying to figure out who he is and where he fits in."

"I'm sure my mother is encouraging him," Blake said as if she hadn't spoken. "She never could deny Charlie anything."

The harsh bitterness in his voice caught Katie off guard. For the second time that evening, she realized what she'd never seen before: Blake was jealous of Charlie. She didn't fully understand it, but she suspected that part of his angry reaction to Charlie's news had more to do with his family relationships than his dislike of anything to do with the Foleys.

Despite his dangerous mood, she felt compelled to comfort him. Beneath his furious reaction there was pain and it drew her to move closer and slip a hand over his shoulder, gently squeezing. "I know how you must feel—"

"No, you don't." He pulled away from her, deliberately putting distance between them again. "Don't pretend you do or that you care."

Katie flinched, hurt by his accusation. "That's not fair or true."

"Isn't it?" Blake stared a moment out the darkened windows then abruptly said, "I need to get out of here."

She almost made the mistake of thinking he meant that they should go together. But he strode over to the coffee table, focusing on gathering up papers and jamming them back into files, and it was obvious he was dismissing her. "I'll call you tomorrow, then," she said quietly, not about to let him see her upset again. "We can finish up anything we've missed."

Getting only a curt nod in answer, Katie grabbed up her purse and her own portfolio and left him, walking fast to where she'd parked her car to avoid the temptation of looking back or worse, turning back.

On the drive back home, she told herself she should be furious with him for more or less throwing her out of his office without so much as an explanation or apology for his behavior. Yet she found herself more worried than angry. She knew Blake well enough to realize he would never treat her that way, even if he was angry with her, unless he was in some sort of emotional turmoil.

Charlie's announcement had bothered him, but his reaction seemed out of proportion. She couldn't define what was bothering him but it seemed to be all tied together with his mother, Charlie, Rex Foley and the whole mess with his business. Maybe part of it, too, was her.

Looking back, she wished she been a little less adamant about turning down his proposition they spend a weekend together. She couldn't accept, not and feel good about herself afterward, but she also couldn't suppress her disappointment with him.

She'd thought they had something more than a basic physical attraction, that they were truly friends, with the potential to be more.

What they were now—if anything—she didn't know.

Skipping the ice and water, Blake drank back his shot of scotch and poured out a second. It wasn't an answer to the memories, the feelings he wanted to obliterate, it didn't even dull them. But after a lifetime of suppressing his emotions instead of acknowledging them, he didn't know any other way.

He wished he'd picked a better place than his study to indulge his misery, though, or at least had bothered to close the door because he'd just raised his second drink when Tate looked in, brow arching at seeing Blake.

"Charlie must have found you," his brother observed, coming in uninvited.

Blake's reply was to finish off his drink and pick up the bottle to pour another.

"This is something you can't take charge of," Tate said. "You can't blame Charlie for wanting to know his father."

"No, I'm supposed to be understanding and accept he's a Foley and support his decision to switch sides. Have I covered it all?" Leaving his drink untouched, Blake paced over to one of the large leather chairs and flung himself down. He didn't like this feeling, that his life was out of control, and there wasn't a damned thing he could do about it.

"This isn't just about Charlie, is it?" Tate asked, coming to sit opposite him. He waited a moment then asked, "Did something happen with Katie?"

"If it did, it doesn't matter any more."

"You're giving up? That doesn't sound like you."

"You're the one who told me I didn't know what I was doing with her. You'll be happy to know you were right."

Tate shook his head. "When you're through wallowing in self-pity, maybe you'll take some advice. Talk to her," he said, without waiting for Blake's agreement. "Admit how you feel. Knowing you and how you prefer keeping everything to yourself, she probably doesn't have any idea."

"What exactly is it I'm supposed to be admitting?" Blake returned.

"I'll let you figure that one out on your own," Tate said. He got to his feet. "It took me a while, but once I got it, I realized it's been there between you two for a long time." Leaving Blake with that cryptic observation, Tate walked out, closing the door quietly behind him.

For a long time afterward, Blake sat alone, staring at nothing, but seeing Katie, wondering if he was honest with himself and with her, if in the end, it would be enough to repair everything that had been torn apart.

Chapter Thirteen

"Tessa," Katie called out as she saw her assistant pass by her office. "Can you please bring me the final hard copy of the menu for the ball?"

Tessa stopped and took a few steps backward to look in at Katie. "Sure. I was going to take it to the printer this morning. Do you still want me to?"

"I need to look it over once more to make certain the changes are all correct. Last time I looked it over a few of the French words had the accents backward and one of the desserts had been entirely left off."

As the impending ball had drawn near, Katie was glad to be able to immerse herself in work. She needed to work to keep from spending all her time lamenting the state of her relationship with Blake.

Tessa bustled back into her office, menu in hand. "Here you go. You do know about the change, right?"

Katie looked up from her computer screen. "What change?"

"Blake made a last-minute change in the menu."

"When did that happen? It took me weeks to put this menu together and do all of the tastings with the chef."

At Katie's sharp tone, Tessa gave an apologetic shrug. "I'm sorry. He told me you wouldn't mind, so I went ahead and made the change."

"I see." *So much for teamwork.* "Well, from now on tell him you have to run everything by me first."

"I will, I just thought that since you two were seeing each other that you'd have already talked it over."

Shoving back from her desk, Katie stood, turned and stared out her window. "No. We haven't." She didn't elaborate. Rehashing the whole mess with Tessa wasn't going to do any good. "I'll call him about this, though. Looking at this menu, I don't understand why he would change the shrimp scampi to prime rib."

"Are you sure you want to talk to him?" Tessa asked, eyeing Katie doubtfully. "If there's a problem, I can call him and ask about this for you."

Katie sighed. "No thanks, I'll talk to him." Even if he were still angry with her, she missed hearing his voice.

After Tessa had left, she delayed making the call, though, barraged with reminders of the last time they'd seen each other. The scene at his office had been so painful in so many ways, for him in regard to Charlie and his mother and for her because she hurt for him. His sexual proposition had only muddied the waters further, making her feel cheap and disposable, like any other of the women with whom he'd had brief flings. But right now, despite all of that, she was missing not only his voice, but their former closeness.

If only they could go back to when their friendship was on the verge of being so much more.

Shaking herself free of her useless musings, she picked up the phone and dialed his cell.

"Hello, Katie," he answered, all cool formality.

"Um…" For a moment she lost her train of thought. Hearing him sound so distant, so guarded after the closeness and passion they'd shared hurt, momentarily throwing her off balance. Then she glanced to her desk, seeing the menu that jogged her mind back on track.

"I'm calling about your menu change. I don't understand why you would switch shrimp for prime rib. I worked it out meticulously with Chef Bedeaux."

"I changed it because several members of my family are allergic to seafood and a number of other people are, as well," Blake explained.

"Oh, I guess I never thought about that."

"You can change it again, if you want to." There was more in his conciliatory tone than in his words. His voice had gentled, sounding almost weary now.

"No, this will be fine. I'm done with revising this menu. It will have to do."

A long awkward silence followed until he broke it with, "Katie, I don't want us to argue. The other day was rough."

A lump rose in her throat. There were so many thoughts and emotions she'd been banking since last they were together, she didn't dare express them now or she'd fall apart crying. "I know," she said softly. "Let's just get through this ball and then we can try to sort everything else out, okay?"

"Okay. I'm willing if you are."

"Of course I am. I just think we need to get past this event before we can focus on anything personal."

"It'll be over soon enough. I'm buried in McCord's business as usual, but please call me or e-mail me if you need any help and I'll drop what I'm doing."

She longed to tell him she needed help now. Not with the ball. With him. With her. With them. Instead she simply thanked him and listened for the click of his phone that ended the call with a sense of loss and the flat sound of emptiness on the other end of the line.

Shoving the pained conversation with Katie from his mind, Blake forced himself to turn his attention back to pressing matters at McCord's, namely, finding the Santa Magdalena Diamond. He hadn't spoken to Paige recently to check on how her hunt for the diamond was progressing—and come to think of it, he'd seen neither hide nor hair of Penny lately, either.

Dialing on his cell, rather than risking using the office line, he connected with Paige. "I haven't heard from you lately. Anything new on the mine?"

"I didn't want to bother you. With the ball being so close, I figured you were up to your ears in last-minute details."

"I am, but this is far more important. Can you talk?"

"Yes. I'm just driving to Café Zozo to have lunch with a friend."

Blake rocked back in his leather chair and whirled it around to gaze out at the Dallas cityscape. "Sorry to interrupt but I haven't seen much of you lately."

There was a pause and then Paige answered. "Well, it's not like you're around much, either. You're with Katie a lot."

"You're mistaken about that. I've scarcely seen Katie in weeks," he said gruffly. He felt suddenly defensive, unwilling to even broach the subject of Katie, afraid his hurt and frustration might seep into his tone of voice. The last thing he wanted was his little sister probing him about his messed up relationship with Katie.

"I'd ask you what was wrong, but I know you wouldn't tell me," Paige said. "You can ask me about the diamond though."

"Okay—any news on the mine?"

Paige's voice brightened. "As a matter of fact, yes. I was able to get to the mine. That's the good news."

"And the bad news?"

"It's old, rickety, unstable. It's going to be a danger-ous venture getting inside and navigating my way to where the diamond is hidden. I'll need to plan carefully and take the right gear with me or I might not make it back out of there."

Silent, Blake considered the risk. It worried him terribly that his sister could wind up trapped in an old collapsing mine. "I don't like the sound of this," he said finally.

"It's okay, really. I'm going to take every precaution. I've been researching how to prepare for and anticipate anything that could happen down there. I've spoken with some old-timers who know the ropes where mine shafts are concerns. They've given me a lot of helpful information."

"Still…"

"I want to do this, Blake. I have to. And I can and I will. For the family."

Blake admired his sister's courage, in fact pride for her welled in him; nonetheless, he wouldn't stop worrying until the whole caper was over and done and she was safely back at home. "We are in desperate circumstances, I won't kid you. We need that diamond if McCord's is to survive."

"I know that. That's why I'm willing to take whatever risk is necessary."

"Promise me one thing."

"What?"

"Don't embark on any of this until you clear everything with me. I want to know every detail of your plan, start to finish. I'll do anything I can to help assure you're safe. Got it?"

"Always the big brother," Paige said flippantly.

"And don't you forget it."

After they'd hung up the phone, it occurred to Blake that Paige wasn't the only one of his siblings that he had lost touch with in the past weeks. He considered a moment then sent Penny a text message asking her to meet with him because he hadn't seen much of her at all. He blamed that on Jason Foley.

I'd love to but I already planned to go to the gym, she wrote back.

Fine. I'll meet you there. We can play a round of racquetball. I'll reserve the court for four.

Penny didn't text back for several minutes. When she did, it didn't sound promising. I was going to do a Pilates class, but I suppose I can skip it today.

Satisfied with his arrangements, Blake arrived at the court on time and began to warm up, pounding the rubber ball with all his might into the back wall. He needed to vent a dozen frustrations over Katie, the family business, worries about Paige, Penny, the elusive Santa Magdalena Diamond, the charity ball, Charlie and his mother.

He slammed the ball again, about ready to give up

on Penny showing. But the door squeaked open and Penny ducked inside, into the white-walled echo chamber of the racquet ball court. Blake caught the ball before it ricocheted off the back wall right at her.

"Wow, that was some serve," she said, hunkering down lest he didn't stop the speeding ball in time.

"You're late."

"I almost didn't come at all."

"Why?"

"Because I have the feeling the reason you asked me here wasn't to play a game." She took her position on the court, rocking from one foot to the other in anticipation of the serve.

A short distance from her, Blake turned to her. "I miss my little sister, isn't that okay?"

"If that's really why you asked me here, of course. It's just not like you."

Avoiding the comment, Blake started the ball in play, and they volleyed some to warm up before keeping score. He knew she didn't have a chance of beating him so he took it easy on her.

"You're patronizing me," she said after winning three shots in a row.

"Would you rather I kill the ball every time?"

Paige shrugged, out of breath. "No. This is challenging enough."

They played hard, shoes squeaking across polished hardwood floors, sweat pouring over Blake's goggles and drenching his shirt. Not realizing they'd run out of time, a pound on the door reminded them their hour was up.

They grabbed their towels, dried off a bit and Blake congratulated Penny on a game well played.

"Thanks for coming," he said. "We don't do enough of this kind of thing together, do we?"

Looking a bit startled, Penny said, "You mean twice a year isn't enough?"

Outside the court Penny started to head for the ladies' locker room but Blake's hand on her arm stopped her. "Come sit with me in the lounge for a minute before we go, would you?"

An apprehensive frown crossed her face, but moments later she agreed to join him. "I've only got a few minutes. I'm scheduled pretty tightly today."

As they walked toward a casual lounge area where guests could watch TV, grab a bite or a drink and chitchat, Blake decided he'd better get to the point quickly before she bolted.

"Seems like you're scheduled pretty tightly every weekend, too. You don't even sleep at home much anymore."

Penny looked away. "I'm an adult. What I do with my time is my business."

Stopping her with a hand to her elbow, he turned her to face him. "Penny, you don't know what you're dealing with in Jason Foley. You don't have much experience and I don't want you to get hurt."

"Thanks, but I can take care of myself. From what I hear, you'd be better off guarding your own heart instead of worrying about mine."

Her words stung sharply but he wasn't about to reveal any emotion in regard to Katie. Instead he merely stared at her, quelling his inner fire.

"Really, Blake, I am sorry but I'm going to be late." She turned on her heel, obviously feeling she couldn't get away from him fast enough. "I have a date with

Jason tonight and I need to go take a shower and start getting ready. We'll do a rematch and have coffee or something another time. Thanks for the game."

Left standing in the foyer of the gym, Blake gave up the idea of sitting in the lounge in favor of a hot shower at home. Now clean, more relaxed and long overdue for a quiet evening, he went to the kitchen to rummage for dinner. The official family dinner hour had passed and with it service from the house staff. He was fine with digging in the fridge and eating in the kitchen breakfast nook, blessedly alone with his newspaper, rather than eating in the usual spot—the formal dining room with everyone hashing over family dramas.

He'd found some leftover roast pork loin and a spicy polenta that smelled too good to be true. Fixing himself a plate and grabbing a bottle of hearty Bordeaux from the wine cooler, he nestled into a window seat to enjoy his solitude.

No sooner than he'd taken the first sip of wine, however, Eleanor padded into the kitchen in her slippers and robe.

Blake groaned inwardly. One night of peace and quiet around here was too much to ask. Tension immediately crawled up his spine and into his head, making it pound.

"What are you doing sitting there eating all alone in the near dark?" she asked, setting a kettle on the stove to boil.

"It seemed like a good idea to me," he said flatly.

"Well, it's not. Not healthy to eat alone. I'll bring my tea and sit with you."

Suddenly the roast pork lost its savory appeal and Blake shoved his plate aside, favoring another glass of wine instead. "Okay."

Eleanor prepared her tea with meticulous ritual,

gracefully carrying the delicate china cup and saucer to the nook where she scooted in opposite Blake.

She bent to sniff the aroma of her brew. "These Asian teas are so fragrant."

"So are these French wines."

Eleanor smiled, glancing at the label. "I recall that vintage." She looked wistful. "It was the year your father and I separated."

Pain rose in her face, tightening her features and hollowing her eyes, making her look suddenly much older. His chest tightened and he realized that if he were ever to forgive his mother for the affair she had with Rex during that separation, he had to understand a whole lot more about her history with him.

There's no time like the present, he heard an inner voice urge. So, bracing himself he acted on it.

"I think it's time you leveled with me. All of this tension, anger and resentment aren't good for any of us. I need to understand about you and Rex Foley. If I don't, I can't even begin to forgive you."

Eleanor gripped her tea cup in both hands, her head dropping as she stared into the steaming cup. When at last she looked up at him again, her eyes were filled with tears.

"I fell in love with Rex when I was sixteen." Swallowing hard, then taking a deep breath, she went on. "We planned to marry," she said, her voice beginning to tremble. "Oh, we were absolutely inseparable for three years, it all seemed so perfect, like a dream come true."

"What happened?" Blake monitored his tone carefully. This was the first time they'd ever spoken of Rex and her past with him and he felt certain it might be the last time she would ever open up. He measured his words. "If you were so in love, why didn't you marry him?"

"It's all so painful," she said. "It all went so wrong. All of our plans..." Bending to sip her tea, she tried again. "One night, after a ridiculous fight with Rex, I was upset. I wanted to punish him for something he'd done that offended me. I can't even remember what that was now. Anyhow, I wanted to make him sorry."

"That sounds pretty typical for a girl that age."

"It was the worst mistake I ever made," Eleanor said grimly. "That night I accepted a date with Devon."

Blake braced himself. The sense that that date changed the course of his mother's life began to settle over him like a shroud.

"Devon had pursued me for months, hoping to take me away from Rex. He saw his moment and he seized it. He made the most of his one chance."

Blake's thoughts turned to Katie, the date she'd had with another man. Had something similar happened? To him, although he was angry, it didn't matter enough to change everything. Had the other man seized his chance with Katie? Right now wasn't the time he could get an answer to that. His mother was about to reveal keys to her past he'd waited a lifetime to have.

"I was very emotional that night, determined to show Rex he couldn't take me for granted, and one thing led to another and, well..." Her eyes turned downward. "Devon and I became intimate." Immediately she lifted her chin, eyes suddenly wide with shame. "I regretted it the moment I gave in. I didn't want it, but it seemed too late. I didn't know how to stand up and say I'd changed my mind. I was still more girl than woman."

Blake reached across the table, briefly touching a hand to hers. "People make mistakes. You should forgive yourself. After all these years, let it go."

Tears began to tumble freely down her pale cheeks. "Blake, that one mistake got me pregnant." She paused, letting the painful truth penetrate him. "In my family, being an unwed teenager wasn't an option. My parents demanded Devon marry me and he happily obliged, in his eyes marking up another victory over the Foleys for the McCords. It was the last thing I wanted but I didn't see any way out of it."

The realization of what she was truly saying began to dawn on Blake and his body went cold. "I'm the result of that *mistake*, aren't I? I'm a mistake."

"Oh, Blake, don't—" Eleanor grasped for his hand and he yanked it back.

"I'm the result of a weak moment on your part with a man you didn't love. While Charlie is the product of your only love." He shook his head. "How could I have been so blind all these years? It makes perfect sense. Everything makes perfect sense now," he said bitterly.

"But I do love you, Blake. Yes, it's been difficult, painful—all that pent up guilt for marrying a man I didn't love, of knowing I ruined my only chance for happiness with Rex in one night." Sobbing now, she couldn't stop herself. "Every time I looked at you…"

"You resented me. I'm the reason you and Rex have been separated all these years." His insides burned, not with anger as much now as with emptiness, loss.

"Blake, please. I tried to hide it, not to take it out on you, but it was hard for me to bond with you, especially since you look so much like Devon. Even now, you remind me so strongly of him and sometimes… Oh, Blake, can you possibly try to understand, to put yourself in my position—to forgive me?"

He stood, unable to bear the sight of her another

moment. It was as if he'd been shot in cold blood but couldn't die. Loneliness, sharper than any dagger's edge, sliced through him. The one person who could help him now, comfort him, the one person he could open up to might have given herself to another man the same way his mother had. He couldn't call Katie. He couldn't talk to his mother or his siblings. All he could do was lock his heart up in a steel cage and toss away the key.

"Don't ask that of me. Not now. Not ever."

Chapter Fourteen

All the months of planning, the focus on each detail, had finally culminated in a perfect evening for the Halloween ball. Katie, standing at the fringe of the crowded ballroom, taking a moment alone to watch the elegant gathering, knew without a doubt that her and Blake's efforts would bring in more funding for the children's hospital than any previous year. They'd sold every ticket to the gala, and the auction sales had far exceeded expectations. It should have been their time to bask in the warm glow of their shared success.

But her smile pasted in place, only half her attention on the conversations around her, Katie's predominant emotion was worry.

"What are you doing alone in a corner?" Her mother's voice pulled Katie out of her thoughts and Katie turned to find Anna at her side.

"After two hours of playing hostess, I needed a break," Katie said lightly. "I think I've managed to talk to every person here at least once."

Anna did a quick study of Katie's face then followed the direction of Katie's gaze, frowning when she spotted Blake. He was standing in a group that included Tate and Tanya, his attention on whatever Tate was saying. "Ah, well, I see…" Anna touched Katie's arm. "I imagine it must be hard seeing Tate with that woman."

"Of course it isn't. Why would it be? I've been telling you for weeks now that you're wrong thinking I'm still pining for Tate."

"Oh, Katie, you've been distracted all evening," Anna said. "I'm not the only one who's noticed. I assumed it was because of Tate and frankly, so has everyone else."

With an impatient shake of her head, Katie dismissed the idea. "That's ridiculous. I'm glad Tate is happy. I wish you would finally give up this idea that I'm in mourning over our broken engagement." Her eyes were drawn back to the group, but it wasn't Tate she sought. Despite her mother's ideas, she'd scarcely noticed him and her gaze skimmed over him now. While her former fiancé and his new love appeared blissful, Blake did not.

She'd been watching Blake most of the evening and he was the cause of her concern. On the surface, he'd played his part of cohost with his usual cool efficiency. At her side, in front of others, he'd openly praised her and had given her the lion's share of the credit for their successes, treating her with a careful courtesy that was minus the warm gestures, the touches she'd grown accustomed to when they were together. He'd made excuses, though, to avoid her beyond what was expected of them as hosts. Despite their agreement to talk things out after the ball, his behavior didn't surprise her, considering the way they'd left things since that night in his office.

But from the moment she'd seen him, she'd known there was something very wrong with him apart from their unresolved issues. Maybe it wasn't obvious to anyone else. To her, though, it was if he were mechanically going through the motions, his mind and heart elsewhere.

"You and Blake are quite the pair tonight," Anna commented with a touch of irritation. "After all the months of work you both spent on this, the two of you are giving the impression you'd rather be anywhere else. I suppose Blake is preoccupied with business," she mused. "All those rumors about McCord's…"

"You should know better than to pay attention to the gossips," Katie told her mother. Whatever was wrong with Blake, she felt sure it wasn't business. Suddenly, she couldn't wait any longer to find out. "I should get back to mingling. I'll find you again later." Quickly kissing her mother's cheek, she headed straight for Blake.

He was alone in the crowd, striding away from the group he'd been a part of in the direction of another. Katie walked up to him, stepping into his path, forcing him to a stop.

"You haven't danced with me," she said without preamble, ignoring the curious glances from bystanders and the surprise that briefly flicked over his face when she clasped his forearm.

"I didn't think I had an invitation," he said, yet there was no emotion in it; it was simply an observation, made absently, as if there were no implications to her asking.

"Now you do."

His lack of question or objections, letting her lead him

into midst of the dancers, increased her uneasiness, though she refrained from saying anything until they were facing each other and pretending to move to the music.

"Blake, what's wrong?" she asked gently.

He didn't meet her eyes, staring at a point over her shoulder. "Why the sudden concern?"

"It's not sudden and you know that. No matter what's happened, I care about you. I can tell you're upset about something. Is it business?"

"I wish it were," he said, so low she almost didn't catch the words.

"What, then?"

She didn't get an answer, not in words. Instead, he looked at her and for brief seconds his mask slipped. Katie caught her breath, taken aback by the pain she glimpsed in his face. She'd never seen him like this, almost vulnerable, as if he'd suffered a crippling emotional blow. It vanished almost immediately, yet left Katie shaken, unable to imagine what had the power to hurt him so deeply.

Avoiding her searching gaze, Blake gathered her closer, his hold tightening, pressing his cheek against her hair.

They finished the dance in silence and as the music ended, Blake released her, taking a step away, his facade firmly in place. "I should get back to—"

"No," Katie said firmly, refusing to let him shut her out this time, "you shouldn't."

"Katie, this isn't the place."

"Then let's find a better place. I'm not above causing a scene," she added quickly, seeing the start of a refusal in his eyes.

Blake looked as if he might challenge her then, his mouth twisting in a sardonic facsimile of a smile, but he relented, sweeping out a hand in a mocking gesture for her to lead the way.

She did, to an isolated nook away from the main ballroom area, in a dimly lit area of the music hall that wasn't being used for the ball. The music and voices faded to a distant sounding hum in the background and she could almost pretend they were completely alone.

Rubbing a hand over his neck, Blake blew out a long breath. "Why are we here?"

"Tell me what's wrong. And don't say it's nothing because I know that's a lie."

"I can't talk about this with you right now."

"Can't or won't?"

"I—can't. I don't even want to think about it. Can you just…" He seemed to flounder for words.

He looked lost and without thinking, Katie put her arms around him and held him close. For a few seconds, he stiffened but, as if he couldn't help himself, then pulled her into a tight embrace.

Katie rested her head on his shoulder and thought about her rejection of his offer to go away, the two of them. Her answer should be the same except right now, Blake needed a friend, whether he wanted to admit it or not. He had no one else in his life willing to offer him comfort and support; certainly no one he would confide in. She wanted to be that person.

Why, she didn't want to admit to herself. It wasn't a lie, telling him she cared. Deep down, though, she knew her reversal was more than that. But she wasn't ready to confront those feelings yet.

Very gently, she leaned inches away from him. "I've changed my mind," she said softly. "Let's go away, just the two of us."

"Katie…" His frown was mixed confusion and suspicion. "You made it clear the other night that isn't what you want."

"It's what I want now. We won't tell anyone, we'll just leave everything behind for a while. Please, Blake—" stretching up, she kissed him, a light press of her mouth on his to stop him from asking more questions "—say yes."

Blake didn't know what to say, let alone think. After all the days apart and the way they'd left things… "Why the change of heart?"

"Because it's something we both need."

"Before—"

"Doesn't matter. We can sort things out later."

Her reasoning didn't entirely satisfy him. In his current state of mind, mistrusting his own judgment, he wondered if the whispers around them were true: that Katie was still smitten with Tate and her attentions to him and her abrupt turnaround was prompted by seeing her former love and his fiancé together.

"I missed you," she murmured, her fingers stroking against his nape. "We both deserve a break, I think."

He translated that to it wouldn't be real; it certainly wouldn't resolve anything. It would be a short-lived fantasy and all too soon they would return to the mess at home. Yet at the lowest point that he could ever recall being, the appeal of escaping with someone he cared about and trusted, even for a little while, was stronger than his reservations.

"Next weekend," he said before he could talk himself out of it. "Gabby's family has a villa on San Vincentia Island. It's private, we'll have the place to ourselves, nothing around but the Mediterranean and a great stretch of beach."

"It sounds perfect." She sighed. "I wish we could leave tonight. The idea of going back in there…"

"I know." It sounded inadequate and the urge to sweep her out a back door, onto his private jet and far away from Dallas to that island paradise was so strong Blake nearly gave in to it. Running away had never been an option for him but at this moment, the temptation to say to hell with everything overrode his dislike of ignoring problems.

Instead of succumbing to it, he took her in his arms again except simply to hold her. It felt like more, though, as if he was holding on to her, grasping at the chance of an anchor in the emotional storm he'd been caught in since his mother's confession. He hated to let go but after a few minutes, aware of the people who had seen them leave and would be speculating about where they'd gone, he gently put her from him.

"We've probably generated enough new gossip for one night," he said.

"Probably. I'm having trouble caring at the moment, though. Blake—" She stopped, opened her mouth to start again, then gave up. Tentatively, she raised a hand, laying it against his cheek, tempting him to lean into her warmth. "Will you be all right?"

It was on the tip of his tongue to say no, but he wouldn't let himself be that weak. "Yes, of course."

By mutual silent agreement, they started walking back to the ballroom, separating almost immediately as they entered the crowd. To onlookers, Blake thought it probably seemed he and Katie were avoiding each other and in a way, at least on his part, it was true.

Exposing his vulnerabilities to her, no matter how briefly, on top of the confrontation with his mother, had yanked his control away, leaving him without a foundation and uncertain how to cope.

He'd never shown weakness to anyone before Katie because he knew it was an invitation for someone to take advantage of him. Yet she hadn't used it against him. She'd listened and held him, and then, inexplicably, she'd changed her mind about them being together.

None of it made sense to him. But he didn't want to analyze anything too closely, for fear the answers he'd get would harder to accept than the questions.

Back amid the noise and what seemed like too many people, Katie wished she'd tried harder to convince Blake to leave the ball, even though she knew it would have been impossible. She wished harder she could have avoided family and friends because it was easier with acquaintances to pretend everything was fine when it wasn't.

"There you are." A well-manicured hand reached out and grasped hers, turning Katie to face Gabby, a beautifully gowned Gabby, sleek in jewel-tone red, but without her handsome spouse at her side. "Back again, I see."

"Have you lost your husband?" Katie asked, hoping to distract Gabby from the questions she was probably dying to ask about her and Blake. She knew it was a vain hope that sharp-eyed Gabby hadn't seen her and Blake disappear together and not return for nearly half an hour.

"He's only very temporarily abandoned," Gabby said easily. "I haven't gotten the chance to talk to you for more than few minutes. So when I saw you standing here all alone—why are you alone, by the way?"

"I don't think being surrounded by a thousand people counts as alone."

Gabby gave up on her attempt at subtlety and asked point-blank, "Where's Blake?"

"Mingling somewhere, I assume," Katie said, at the same time hunting around for a safer topic. Committed now, she was nonetheless starting to second-guess her impulsive decision to go away with Blake. More daunting was her fear that she agreed not out of concern or caring or friendship, but because she'd fallen in love with him.

She'd fallen in love with him....

She loved him.

"It's true, then. You two are together."

Katie looked at Gabby and her friend smiled knowingly.

"Did you just figure it out?" Gabby asked.

"It's not what you're thinking."

"Oh, I think it's exactly what I'm thinking."

"Honestly, do you think between my past with Tate and all the other complications we would ever end up— together?" She had wavered so much, afraid of making a mistake, unsure of what she wanted. She didn't believe Blake was dedicated to exploring any possibilities with her beyond friendship and a casual brief affair—at least not any more.

"It doesn't matter what I think, or anyone else, either," Gabby said. "This is between you and Blake."

"Whatever *it* is."

"I did warn you any relationship with Blake wouldn't be easy."

"Maybe it wouldn't be so hard if I had a clue what I'm doing," Katie blurted out. She pressed fingertips to her forehead. "I sound about seventeen."

Gabby laughed. "No, just confused. Love will do that to you. If it's any consolation, Blake has no clue what he's doing, either. My advice is the two of you should get out of here and work on trying to figure it out."

It was so near to what she and Blake did plan on doing—at least the escape part—that Katie wondered if Gabby somehow knew. Considering Gabby's talent for ferreting out information, it wouldn't surprise her.

"Speaking of getting out of here," Gabby said, "it's time I got back to my man and let you find yours."

Katie let Gabby leave without correcting her; Blake wasn't hers and wasn't likely to be anytime soon. But she couldn't deny she wanted him; in some ways it felt as if she always had.

That didn't stop her from anticipating and fearing a broken heart. She loved him and this weekend away was as likely to turn out badly, as it was to fix anything between them.

Yet she wasn't ready to give up the time she and Blake could spend together, no matter how brief. It had been too long, if ever, that she'd allowed her emotions full rein and damn the consequences. She wasn't going to let the opportunity slip away, not when it meant so much.

Not when there was a small hope that, despite everything, there was still a chance for them.

It was nearly two when Blake let himself into the McCord mansion, feeling the weight of too many sleepless nights, the long drawn-out evening, and his own thoughts in the stiff set of his shoulders and neck. He almost hated coming back here, having to live with the pervading tension between him and his mother, though they'd done a good job of staying out of each other's way the past week and even tonight. His only solace was in a couple of days, he could escape with Katie, at least for a short time.

Shedding his jacket and tie as he went, he started toward his room, only to be stopped by a quiet voice.

"You're finally home." Eleanor stood in the archway of the living room, still in her formal gown.

"I couldn't leave until everyone else had," he said shortly, adding, "What are you doing up?" though he guessed she'd been waiting for him.

"I wanted to talk to you."

Blake scrubbed a hand over his face. "Tonight? Can't it wait?"

"If we wait, we'll both continue to find some reason to avoid it." Eleanor gestured toward the living room and Blake, too weary—emotionally and physically—to argue, followed her in.

He tossed his jacket and tie on a chair, unfastening the first few buttons of his shirt, but stayed standing as his mother took a seat opposite him. "I don't need to ask what this is about."

"I can't tell you how many people came up to me tonight and asked if there was something wrong with you," Eleanor said instead of answering him.

"Am I supposed to apologize for that?" Hearing the bitterness in his voice, he shook his head sharply. "It's easy enough to tell them it's business. It's even partly the truth."

"That's not the point. Blake…" She half raised a hand then let it drop. "I don't want to leave things like this between us. Despite what you may think of me, I care about you and I hate seeing you in pain and knowing I'm the cause."

"I don't want to leave it like this, either, but frankly I don't know how to fix it." He didn't add that he wondered if it could be fixed. There was no way for his mother to take back her confession, no way for him to forget it. "I'm going away for a couple of days," he said abruptly.

Eleanor's brows raised. "On business?"

"No, it's not business."

"I see," she responded, although she sounded doubtful. Yet she didn't press him for an explanation. "It's not like you just to leave. I can't recall you ever taking a vacation."

"I need to get away." There was a long silence between them and then Blake blew out a breath. "This isn't going to be resolved tonight. When I get back— we'll talk then. Maybe…" He tried to think of a compromise, a way he could learn to live with knowing there was a time she'd wished he'd never been born. Nothing came to mind and he settled for "Maybe a few days away will help me clear my head."

"I hope, for your sake, that it does," Eleanor said. She rose to her feet and after a moment's hesitation, came up to him and touched his arm. "Blake…"

The open concern in her face was almost as difficult to take as her admissions because part of him wanted to believe it was honest, while the hardened side of him rejected it as guilt. "I can't do this right now," he said repeating what he'd told Katie. "I— I'll talk to you in a few days."

He turned on his heel and quickly left the room.

Chapter Fifteen

Blake stood on the patio of the elegant villa—the late-afternoon sunlight glittering on the clear blue of the Mediterranean, blazing against the sky, the air perfumed with sea and lush clusters of bright red bougainvilleas—and was unmoved by the vista of paradise. It seemed a lifetime ago he'd wanted this, days isolated with Katie in a sensual hideaway. Bringing her to San Vincentia should have fulfilled one of his fantasies. Instead, he felt detached from it all, unable to shake off the shadows of Dallas.

A whisper of sound turned him from the view and Katie walked over to him, leaning her hands against the low railing to look out at the sea. Barefoot, she'd changed into a sleeveless white dress and the light breeze molded the thin material to her curves, taunting him by revealing she wore little underneath. When she stretched and turned her face up to let the sun kiss her skin, Blake decided paradise was overrated. The view couldn't compete with the vision of Katie.

"It's beautiful, isn't it?" she said, taking in a long breath. "This is definitely one of your better ideas."

"Do you want a drink?" he asked abruptly and was already starting inside before she answered.

She glanced at him, brows slightly raised, and shook her head. "No, thank you. Not now."

He was being a bastard and he knew it, had been since they'd left Texas and the whole of the plane trip to Italy, the boat ride to the island, and up to this moment. Though he didn't deserve it, Katie had put up with his moodiness and hadn't pressed him for an explanation. Pouring out a generous portion of scotch, Blake drank it back, taking the second one with him out onto the patio.

Katie didn't comment, but the look she slanted him told him she wanted to. Finally, she moved to his side and slid her hand up his arm to the crux of his neck and shoulder, very lightly massaging the tight muscle. "It's good to be away from everything."

"Yes, for as long as it lasts."

"Blake—"

He looked at her and seeing the determination in her eyes, knew she wasn't going to accept cryptic answers and rebuffs from him anymore.

"Be honest with me," she said. "I know something is wrong and it's more than our issues. I want to help but I can't do that if you won't talk to me. What happened, before the ball?"

For long seconds, he balked, thought about the things he'd have to tell her to fulfill his promise to be honest. "I'm sorry for the way I've been acting," he substituted.

"It's not been fair to you. But it has nothing to do with you, I promise."

"Then what does have to do with?"

Blake nearly refused to tell her; it meant dragging out the memories again and they were too fresh to be painless. The gentle encouragement in her voice, though, broke his resolve to guard his feelings. They were alone and if there was one person he could trust to understand, it was Katie.

"Do you know who I am?" he asked. He gripped the railing hard enough to leave marks, his knuckles whitening with the effort. "I'm the reason my mother and Rex Foley have been separated all these years. I was never supposed to be a McCord, or to be at all, for that matter."

Her fingers tightened on his shoulder. "I don't understand."

"I didn't, either, until recently." He told her then, all of it, not gilding it with emotions or his mother's excuses, but reciting it starkly. When he was done, he waited, expecting her surprise, questions, or worse, pity. What he didn't anticipate was the flare of anger in her eyes.

"How could Eleanor say those things to you?"

"I suppose she felt compelled to explain, or maybe justify what she'd done." Blake pushed a hand through his hair. "Hell, I don't know."

"There isn't any justification for telling your child he was unwanted and resented," Katie said hotly.

"At least I understand why I was never her favorite son. It explains a lot of things."

"It doesn't make it easier to accept," she said in a voice suddenly very quiet.

She made to put her arms around him, but Blake quickly shifted out of her reach. "This was a mistake. I shouldn't have brought you here, not like this. Not because I don't want to be with you," he added quickly, seeing the hurt flash into her eyes. "You don't know how much I want that."

"Then why—"

"As my mother pointed out, I'm too much like my father. I wanted you and I didn't bother to consider your feelings when I asked you to go away together. I assumed you'd say yes. I convinced myself that's all we'd ever have together, that you weren't any better than any other woman I've known." There was more he had to say and it felt like the hardest thing he'd ever done. Exposing his vulnerabilities was almost as painful as reciting his confrontation with his mother. "I always thought you were too good for Tate. But you're too good for me, as well. I can't believe I could ever be the kind of man you deserve."

Katie's eyes were shining with unshed tears. "What about what you deserve?" She didn't give him time to come up with any good answer for that. "Success and ambition are poor substitutes for loving and caring."

He knew that, didn't he?

"You expect too much of yourself," she began, closing the space between them, slowly, as if she were afraid he'd bolt if she got too near. "I don't need perfection, Blake. And you aren't your father, you never could be."

"Then I'm doing a pretty good imitation."

"Not even close." Katie ignored his move to evade her and laid her palm against his face, her caress warm and tender. "You're so much better than that."

It was tempting, so tempting, to grasp her close, satisfy a base desire as a poor substitute for a deeper emotional need. She would be willing. But he didn't want her offering herself like a consolation prize. A few days of being her lover wasn't going to be enough.

The slight pressure of her fingers recaptured his gaze. "Blake, what are we doing here? I thought I knew. But now—I'm not sure."

"I don't think either of us has ever been sure of what we were doing."

"No, but I need to know."

If the circumstances were different, if his defenses hadn't been lowered and he'd been in control of his emotions, he would have given her the easy, glib answer. He couldn't. Compared to the possibility of another rejection, lying to her suddenly seemed the worst he could do.

"When I found out about you and Marcus," he started slowly, "I didn't expect to feel like you'd betrayed me. But I did."

"I felt the same way, but it wasn't like that."

"I know. Even if it was, I didn't have the right to be jealous, of him—or Tate."

That startled her. "Tate?"

He took her hand, guiding it down from his face but lacing their fingers, unable to stop touching her. "It was hell, watching you with him, knowing you loved him—and wishing it was me."

"You? But…you never—" She shook her head as if what he'd admitted didn't make any sense. "Why didn't you ever say anything?"

"What was I supposed to say? That I'd fallen in love with my brother's fiancée? That all those nights I knew you were with him, I wanted to be the one in your bed?"

"If I had known—"

"Then what? You were making wedding plans, Katie. You said you were in love and that you were happy. I doubt you would have thanked me for telling you I thought you were making a mistake." Letting go of her hand, he fisted his hands over the railing again. "You keep telling me you're not sure how you feel or what you want. If I'd said anything then, it would have caused complications none of us was ready to deal with."

"Maybe that was true then," Katie confessed, "but not anymore."

"Isn't it? It's still complicated."

"Probably, although right now, it doesn't feel like it. Blake..." The softly spoken request implicit in her voice compelled him to face her. "I love you. I've never been more certain of anything."

He could have argued or questioned except she stepped up and pressed her mouth to his and in that instant, swept aside his doubts, leaving him with the fantasy turned reality of having Katie where he'd wanted her for years: in his arms and in love.

It happened so fast, a dizzying rush of sensation and emotion released by his admission, that Katie could only hold tightly to Blake and let it overwhelm her. It was as if all these years she'd been blind and suddenly she could clearly see everything they both had denied for so long.

Since that first forbidden kiss after the Labor Day party, she'd known, though she'd refused to admit, that Blake wasn't simply a friend. He was the man who'd always been there for her, waiting, though for the longest while all she'd seen was Tate's older brother, not a would-be lover. Now, she didn't want them to waste any more time avoiding their feelings, arguing, talking and pretending it wasn't inevitable they'd be lovers.

Leaning into him, she let her lips tell him how much she needed him.

Blake eased his arms around her, returning her kiss but his was more tender than passionate—an affirmation of love rather than desire. The care he took touched her yet she sensed he was deliberately holding himself in check. Accustomed to him taking the lead, his hesitation, lack of confidence almost, concerned her but she thought she understood. He was afraid of repeating his father's sins, taking advantage of her vulnerabilities to get what he wanted.

She was determined to convince him the difference was love.

"Are you going to make me beg?" she teased with a brush of her lips against his ear.

Instead of returning her light tone, he shifted a few inches back, looking troubled. "Too much more of this and it'll be the other way around. But we don't have to take this any further if you're not sure it's what you want."

"What does a girl have to do to convince you?"

"Katie—" Framing her face in his hands, Blake looked into her eyes, his reflecting an intense emotion that both excited and humbled her. "I love you. I should have told you a long time ago."

"Show me," she urged. "Please, Blake." And spurred by the open desire on his face, she began unbuttoning his shirt. "This is right. I know it is."

Her certainty overpowered his hesitation. He gathered her to him, kissing her in an imitation of how she wanted him to love her and she moved restlessly in his arms, wanting to give him everything, craving what only he could give her in return. The low hum of pleasure he made deep in his throat intensified the feeling, sharpening the edges of her need for him.

He honed it further, exploring the hollows and curves of her neck and shoulders, his mouth replacing his hands as he pushed down the thin straps of her dress.

Katie encouraged him, spreading open his shirt, splaying her fingers over his chest, suddenly greedy for the hard press of his body against hers. She ached, in a way she never had before with Tate or anyone. From their first kiss to now, being with Blake was all heat and need; there was no room for thought other than she wanted more.

As though she'd asked aloud, he granted her wish, reclaiming her mouth, his tongue sliding along hers at the same time he ran his hands over her back, up her sides, until his fingers brushed her breasts. His thumbs grazed the sensitive tips through the thin cotton of her dress and her breath caught, released as she breathed his name.

She felt, rather than saw, his smile, and he continued to stroke and tease her a little longer before murmuring in her ear, "Let's go inside." His arm was around her waist and he'd made a motion in the direction of the door before he realized she wasn't going with him.

Katie glanced around them. The patio was on two levels overlooking the sea, the steps leading down from the upper level where they stood to a swimming pool, tiled all around in a bright mosaic. A small smile curved her mouth and she took Blake's hand. "Let's not."

"If this is another one of your fantasies," he said, following her down the steps to the pool's edge, "I like it."

"There is one problem." She pretended to frown.

"And that is…?"

"I don't have a swimsuit."

"That's okay." His gaze swept over her, hot enough to make her flush. "Neither do I."

Blake cut off any further words by kissing her, long and deep. Without breaking contact with her mouth, he eased down the zipper of her dress, sliding the material off her body until it pooled at her feet and left her wearing only a lacy white thong. Halting to look at her, the almost dumbstruck expression in his eyes had her smiling to herself.

"I don't know if you've heard this enough," he said huskily, "but I guarantee that in my lifetime, I won't stop telling you. You're the most beautiful thing I've ever seen." Watching intently, he lightly dragged his fingertips over her lips, tracing a path down her throat, to the valley between her breasts.

Then, as if the feel of her skin under his broke his patience, he dropped to one knee, teasing her with nibbling kisses on her stomach as he drew down the thong. Tossing it somewhere behind him, he slid his hands back up her legs, shaping her thighs and hips, the caress of his hands and mouth becoming more intimate as—giving this self-appointed task the same focused, meticulous attention he gave anything he considered important—he discovered what she liked and what she needed. Pleasure spiked in her and she gripped his shoulders, gasping at the riot of sensation.

He made her tremble and burn and forget there was ever anyone else before him. Finally, knees weak and threatening to buckle, she traced the line of his jaw, drawing his eyes to hers and took one small step back toward the pool.

In answer to her silent invitation, he quickly stood, shedding his shirt at the same time he slanted his mouth over hers. Somewhere in between kisses he managed to strip off the rest of his clothes, but he only gave her scant moments to appreciate the subtle definition of muscle and long, lean lines of his body. Scooping her off her feet, he carried her into the pool and braced himself against the side before drawing her to him.

The sun-warmed water complemented the sensuous slide of skin to skin. Breath ragged, his mouth hungry on hers, Blake's hands roved over her back to her hips and in one fluid motion, he lifted her up, her legs wrapped around his waist and her arms around his neck. Their gazes locked and she shifted her hips to meet his thrust, pushing forward to take him even deeper inside.

Maybe it was cliché, and maybe it was simply love, but for the first time in her memory, a sense of completion swept over her. This was what she'd been missing, the overwhelming combination of desire and pure feeling that she'd dismissed as a romantic ideal. With Blake, it was vividly real.

They made love to each other, partners in this, too. Blake set the first slow stroking rhythm, loving her with a passion so interwoven with emotion it brought her to tears. Then he let her lead and she tried to give him back the same, to warm the cold places in him and replace painful memories with ones of her willingly yielding heart and body to him. Finally, close to the edge and teetering there, the ache of anticipation prolonged by his skillful touch, she fell, crying out his name.

And as he always had been, he was there to catch her.

A slender leg hooked over his and slim fingers trailed over his chest and stomach, twitching down the edge of the sheet that barely covered them both.

Without opening his eyes, Blake turned his head to kiss Katie's temple and murmured, "Were you planning on eating and sleeping this weekend, or is this the only activity on the agenda?"

"Are you complaining?" A few more inches of sheet retreated at the nudge of her hand. They'd made love twice in the pool before moving indoors, promising each other a shower and dinner. Hours later, they'd yet to even glance in the direction of the kitchen.

"No," he assured her, "just contemplating my odds of survival."

She laughed, the rich, happy sound vibrating against his skin. "I have faith you're up to the challenge. We have a lot of lost time to make up for."

Blake shared that sentiment but he was still trying to work out how he'd ended up with her in his life. Making love with Katie had been so much more than he'd expected or ever experienced; being in love with Katie and her loving him was unbelievable. Unbelievable and daunting. She was the first person he'd let behind his walls and now that she'd gotten under his skin and lodged in his heart, he didn't dare imagine what it would be like without her.

"I don't want to lose this," he said, unaware he'd voiced the thought aloud until she propped herself up on her elbow to look questioningly at him.

"This—" she inched her hand lower on his body "—or..."

"You. I don't want to lose you." In a sudden motion, he rolled toward her so they were face-to-face. "I can't believe I almost messed this up. What scares me is that I know I could screw things up again."

"I'm scared I could do the same thing," she confessed. "I guess there aren't any guarantees. But I love you, Blake, and I'm willing to take that chance."

"Me, too," he said softly. Very gently, he drew his fingertips over her cheek, relearning the curves and the texture of her skin. "What amazes me is you've seen the worst of me and you're still here."

"You're forgetting something."

"And that is?"

Katie tugged the sheet completely aside and fitted her body to his. "I've seen the best, too."

Unable to resist even if he'd wanted to, Blake bent and kissed her and for a long time afterward, his world narrowed to a bed in paradise and loving her.

The planned four-day retreat stretched into six, and then ten and it wasn't until Blake realized that it had been almost two weeks since he'd bothered to check his messages or e-mail or even thought about his responsibilities that he reluctantly brought up the subject of leaving. They were sitting together on the beach, watching the sunset, the surf lapping at their feet, and Dallas seemed a million miles away.

"I imagine by now your family and mine are convinced we've disappeared for good," he said. He rested his forehead against the tangled silk of her hair, breathing in the mingled scent of wind and sea and her musky perfume. "I suppose we should have called at least once."

Katie's sigh echoed with longing. "I wish we could stay. Knowing what's waiting at home…" She left it unsaid but Blake all too well understood her desire to make their escape permanent.

"It's tempting—"

"But we can't." Leaning her head back on his

shoulder, she lightly kissed the side of his neck then fixed her eyes on the horizon where the last of the day's sun had painted the sky in pink and orange. "I just don't want things to change."

"They won't," he said, the edge to his words betraying his own worries that once they were back home, the love she professed for him wouldn't be strong enough to withstand reality and his bubble of happiness would irreparably burst. "Not unless you want them to."

"No," she said softly and twisted to face him, "I don't. Do you?"

"No," he repeated and it was a vow. He punctuated it with a brush of his lips to hers.

"Then I guess we're going home."

The finality in her voice convinced him to act on a sudden impulse. "What would you say to playing hooky for a few more days?"

"Here?"

"In Paris." He'd succeeded in surprising her and he smiled. "There's a private dealer who has a collection of canary diamonds I'm interested in buying. We could stay a few days there—" he slowly traced his fingertips along the edge of the cotton camisole she wore, rewarded by the faint flush coloring her fair skin "—combine business with pleasure."

She smiled back, her eyes alight again with the happiness he'd grown accustomed to seeing in the last two weeks. "If I didn't know you better, I'd say you were making up this whole story about buying diamonds just to get me to say yes."

"Is it working?"

Her arms snaked around his neck and right before she kissed him, she murmured, "Oh, yes."

Chapter Sixteen

Katie peered out of the window of the jet, hoping to catch her first glimpse of the Eiffel Tower. Her fingers were laced with Blake's and she gave his hand a quick squeeze. "Isn't it funny that as much as I've traveled in Europe, I've never been to Paris?"

"Apparently your first time was supposed to be with me."

She turned away from the window. "Was it?" she asked, reading a double meaning into his words that she wasn't sure he intended.

"Never doubt it."

"Are we still talking about Paris?"

"I don't know," Blake said, leaning in to nuzzle her neck, "are we?"

The look of disbelief she put on wasn't entirely false. "Are you telling me that Blake McCord, the man who thinks he can control everything, believes in destiny?"

"Only when it comes to you. But don't tell anyone. It'll ruin my image."

This side of Blake—loving, teasing, content to forget about responsibilities, *happy*—made Katie fall in love with him all over again. At the same time, she wondered if she was deluding herself by believing they would last once they were back in Dallas. They hadn't talked about the future beyond Paris except in vague terms. He loved her, she knew, and he'd promised her things between them wouldn't change. But did that mean he wanted her permanently in his life and if he did, as what…his friend, lover, or—

She stopped herself. No matter how much she liked the sound of forever, she couldn't assume Blake felt the same. For now, she determined to treasure their time together, however long it lasted, and face reality when she had to.

"Have I lost you?" Blake's voice, a little husky, pulled her eyes to his.

"Of course not," she returned lightly. "I was just thinking of all the ways we could enjoy Paris." Finding his lips, she gave him a slow, thorough kiss. "Thank you for bringing me here. I can't think of a better way to extend our escape."

"The pleasure's mine," he said. He searched her face and she expected questions about her distraction. Instead, he nodded to the window. "You might want to look out again. We should be almost right over the city."

She ignored the outside vista, her view of him more tantalizing. "The most romantic city in the world."

"So I've heard—" and as he said it he gathered her into his arms "—we'll have to put it to the test."

He drew her into a kiss, opening her mouth under his, and Katie forgot about Paris and her doubts. She was on the verge of suggesting they start their testing while they were still in the clouds, but the sounds of footsteps stopped her.

The flight attendant, the only one aboard Blake's private jet, approached to check that their safety belts were fastened for landing. Katie was thankful that for most of the trip the woman had stayed discretely invisible as it was clear she and Blake preferred privacy.

"We'll be landing at Charles de Gaulle in a few minutes. Your car will be waiting in the usual place, Mr. McCord. Jean-Paul will be your driver, as you requested."

"Excellent," Blake said, his arm still around Katie, "and thank you."

The pretty young blonde ducked away and Katie, regretting the interruption, resumed her search out the window for landmarks she might recognize. "I'd hoped to see Notre Dame from up here. I've wanted to see it since I was a little girl."

"You won't, but you will see it from down there. We're staying in the Latin Quarter. The cathedral is close by. I opted for a small, elegant Parisian boutique hotel over one of the overblown tourist draws."

Katie laid her head on his shoulder. "Mmm…sounds perfect to me."

The plane landed smoothly and like clockwork Jean-Paul was on hand to gather their luggage and whisk them into the limo. On the drive to the hotel, Blake held her close to his side, pointing out historical and architectural markers, punctuated here and there with a kiss or an intimate touch, making it difficult for her to keep her mind on Paris.

"They drive here like they do in Rome," she said as they swung around a roundabout and she landed halfway onto Blake's lap.

"Ah, but there can be benefits to that." He took the opportunity to graze his fingers over her thigh, fully bared when her skirt followed the car's sharp turn.

"Is this why you asked for Jean-Paul?" she asked, pretending modesty by putting a few discreet inches between them, "because you enjoy the benefits of his driving skills?"

Blake laughed. "You have to admit, it makes the drive more interesting."

"I can tell I'm not going to be seeing much of the city," she teased, laughing herself. She glanced outside at the passing scenery. One after another, each more charming than the last, the small, quaint restaurants were just beginning to show signs of preparing for the evening service with waiters, clad in dark clothes and white aprons, changing table linens and candles, putting out handwritten menus for passersby to peruse. "This is a maze of streets. I could never find my way out of here."

"Good. Then I know if I decide to keep you here forever, you're stuck with me."

She answered with a nod, the implication of *forever* one she didn't want to contemplate right now.

"Here we are." Blake nodded ahead to a stone building several stories high, each level boasting colorful window flower boxes and royal blue awnings. "Hôtel Saint-Jacques, one of my favorites."

As Jean-Paul organized the luggage, a liveried servant greeted Blake personally. He introduced Katie and the concierge bowed. "We are at your service, *mademoiselle*. Anything you desire, you have but to ring down for me."

Katie smiled at the dashing older gentleman who stood about four inches shorter than she. *"Merci, monsieur,"* she said, then complimenting him on his charming-looking hotel, delighted him with her perfect French.

"I didn't know you spoke French," Blake said as they followed a bellman to the front desk.

"Part of a proper lady's education, or so my mother insisted."

He leaned close to her ear. "I'd like to be your teacher for an *improper* education."

Her lips curved in a seductive smile and she murmured back, "Who says it wouldn't be the other way around?"

"If it involves learning about your champagne fantasy," he commented just as they were about to step into the elevator and loud enough for the bellman to overhear, "then you're got my complete and undivided attention for a lesson."

The bellman smirked and Katie shook her head at Blake, although her heart wasn't in the reprimand. Instead, she had a sudden explicit image of them together and all the creative ways she could change his mind about not liking champagne.

The heat between them flared as they squeezed into the tiny elevator, her breasts pressed to his chest, the two of them, the bellman and their luggage barely fitting as the ornate iron door closed. By the time the bellman opened the door to their top-floor suite, the passion between them was palatable.

"Oh, Blake, this is wonderful," Katie breathed, taking in the lavishly appointed rooms, decorated in rich jewel-toned fabrics and priceless-looking antiques. She walked over to the window. "And look at the view, the river— I can't imagine anything more beautiful."

"I can." The bellman gone, Blake strode to her side and pulled her to him, running his hands over her body as though he'd been starving for her.

"You'd think we've been waiting for weeks for this," she said, already yielding to the delicious pleasure.

"It feels like it. I can't seem to get enough of you." Cupping his hands on her bottom, he lifted her until she wrapped her legs around his waist. Her skirt scrunched up, revealing black lace thigh highs and slender legs. Blake carried her to the master bedroom, kissing her feverishly as they moved.

Gently he bent and laid her back on the bed, long legs partially spread where they met his thighs. "You're just too beautiful," he said, his expression almost reverent as his gaze swept her body.

"I didn't know that was possible."

"Neither did I. Until I saw you like this."

Katie started to sit up, to touch him, but Blake bent over her, and taking her wrists in his hands, carefully opened her arms at each side and laid her back onto the comforter. "No, let me." Sliding off his jacket, he moved over her and with torturous deliberation, unfastened each button of her blouse, kissing every new appearance of skin as he went.

Her instinct was to reach for him, for his shirt, follow his lead, but again, when she lifted her arms to do so, he took her wrists and pressed them back onto the bed. "Not yet."

Heat tingled through her, an excitement in letting herself be guided by him, of giving herself up to his explorations, unable to respond or return his touch. It was a delicious frustration, growing by the moment as his hands found her waist and pulled her blouse from her skirt, exposing her breasts to him. With a slow, teasing tongue and skillful teeth, he drew back the layer of satin and lace covering one breast, giving him access to her soft flesh. At the same time, he stretched out his arms, laying his hands atop hers, palm to palm and lightly pressing them to the bed.

Katie sucked in a ragged breath and he moved to lavish her other breast with similar attention. All the while, his body hovered over hers, just out of reach. His thighs against the end of the bed kept her legs separated, in a position that left her craving more, aching for him to lie fully on her and take her to heights she knew they could reach together.

But Blake was determined to continue his now wonderfully agonizing seduction. Unclasping the front fastener on her bra, he inched his way with light flickering kisses, across and around her breasts, down her chest and to her belly, where he paused to take longer tastes of her skin.

She moaned in anticipation of what he would do next. "Are you trying to kill me?" she managed, gasping as his tongue flicked a particularly sensitive spot.

"Don't worry," he promised with a wicked smile, "I won't let you die unsatisfied."

Lifting himself farther from her, he released her hands, then cupping his hands beneath her back he brought her off the bed far enough to remove her shirt and bra. All that remained were her skirt, shoes, stockings and underwear and she itched to sit up to rip them off.

Blake, however, made it clear he intended to do that for her. Easing his palms down her hips and thighs, to raise her skirt up so he could remove her stockings, he continued all the way to her feet. There he bent and knelt at the foot of the bed, carefully slipping the straps off her black heels, one by one, then removing first one shoe then the other and tossing them with exaggerated finesse to the side of the room.

Katie laughed and so did he. But when she began to rise off the bed to wrap her arms around him, his hands found hers, entwining their fingers and pressing her back down slowly, softly into the comforter. "Didn't they teach you that patience is a virtue?"

Her body sensitized now to his every movement, each brush of his hand or lips, she felt herself softening for him. "There's nothing virtuous about you, or this. You're not playing fair," she said breathlessly as he slipped one stocking down her thigh, tracing after it with his tongue.

As he flung the stocking out to land on a nearby chair, he smoothed his hands slowly along the length of her leg, from her toes, feet, ankles, calves and thighs all the way under her skirt to lightly grasp her bottom. Repeating the ritual with the other stocking and leg, this time when he reached her backside, he continued on to find the zipper of her skirt. In one fluid motion, the skirt fell open and slid from her body, leaving only her black lace thong to cover her.

He stood over her, an appreciative but hungry look pooling in his eyes. With painstaking slowness, he unbuttoned his shirt, pulled it from his waist and tossed it aside. She lifted her head to look at him, marveling once more at the ripples in his chest and abs, yearning to clasp his arms and pull him down onto her.

But, then again, Blake's game did have its rewards, and watching him as he started stripping off his clothes was definitely one of them. When he'd finished, he surprised her, moving back a step, and taking her thighs in his palms, switched places, opening his legs to move hers together between his thighs. He pressed her legs close as he again began a taunting exploration, with lips and this time hands, of her breasts, belly and below,

"I am going to die, you know," she panted, unable to stop herself any longer from squirming with desire. Still, he held her legs closed, anchored between his.

She reached for his neck, trying to pull him down to her, but he flattened her palms to the sides at the same time unexpectedly, he suddenly reversed his legs, moving one knee then the other between hers to open her thighs to him. All the while, the rest of his body balanced above her, just out of reach.

He stayed there, obviously enjoying her pleasured torment, until finally leaning close enough for her to feel the intimate brush of him against her wet heat.

"Now, Blake, please—"

He ignored her, toying with her, going no further than a teasing touch, drawing back and repeating the motion.

"You're going to pay for this."

"Is that a promise or a threat?"

Lifting her legs, she wrapped them around his waist and, locking them, pulled him to her with all of her strength. "Definitely a promise."

"Touché," he said, with a sexy laugh and finally, he gave them what they both wanted, joining them together, loving her with the passion that had been building since they stepped onto the jet hours and hours ago.

The tension between them, stretched to the breaking point by Blake's sensual play, found release in their lovemaking, and when she finally fell apart in his arms, calling out his name, Katie decided an eternity in Blake's arms wouldn't be enough.

* * *

When he awoke, tangled in the sheets, clothes strewn everywhere and forgotten, their room was dark. Sounds of laughter and the glow of gas lamps and restaurant lights filtered up to their window and Blake had to remember where they were.

"Paris," he whispered to a still-sleeping Katie, "the city of love."

With a tender kiss to her cheek, he brushed a curl of dark hair from her beautiful face and watched, smiling, as she sighed and snuggled closer, marveling at how she'd changed him. She'd saved him from himself and loving her was no longer enough. He wanted more. He wanted her with him, not for a few stolen weeks, but always.

They were in Paris and in love, the ideal circumstances to convince her they belonged together. He'd pulled off plans against stiffer odds. And he'd never been more determined to succeed now.

Katie stirred, her eyes fluttering open, her lips rounding into a contented smile as she focused on him. "Good morning," she murmured.

He smiled back, bending to kiss her. "Actually, it's good night."

"Guess I lost track of the time."

"Me, too, but my stomach didn't. I'm starving. How about you?"

"I'm not awake enough to know yet, but I'm sure once I get up I'll feel it."

"What do you say we throw on some clothes and go grab dinner while they're still serving?"

"Well…" She stretched languorously. "That would involve moving from this bed."

"And—?"

In a quick motion that belied her seeming lack of motivation, she sat up, sliding a leg over him so she straddled his hips. "And I've decided I'm hungry. If you're still serving, that is."

"For you, always," he vowed and for a long time, dinner was forgotten.

The next morning, though, Blake promised himself he wouldn't let anything—Katie included—distract him from his plans. He wanted everything to be perfect for her.

He called for room service and they finally abandoned the bed to breakfast at a small café table near their window, people watching below as they ate croissants and cheese and fruit and drank espresso.

"I thought we'd visit a few landmarks today," he said as they were finishing. "Notre Dame in particular, since that's first on your list."

"Weren't you supposed to be here on business?" she reminded him, her eyes bright with mischief.

"Tomorrow," he said, dismissing work in a word. "Today I want to spend with you." He leaned across the table to briefly touch a kiss to her lips. "Everything I want to show you is pretty close by and we could take the limo, but you'll get a better feel for the city if we walk and take the trains. Unless you'd rather drive."

"Now I'm getting worried." Katie eyed him over the rim of her cup.

"Worried?"

"Yes, because I think I left the real Blake McCord in Dallas. It's been two weeks, you haven't cared about business, and I'm pretty sure if I asked, you'd agree to stay here indefinitely. Not that I don't like the change, mind you," she added and he could tell from the twitch of her lips and the light in her eyes she was teasing him, "but I'm wondering what brought all this on."

He didn't have to wonder. "I love you," he said simply.

All the amusement went out of her expression and she looked directly at him and pronounced softly, "I love you, too."

That brought him out of his seat to take her in his arms and kiss her, slowly, a caress layered with passion and tenderness and the promise of many more to come. When it ended, he held her close for long moments before at last she tilted her head back to smile at him.

"If we're going to do all this sightseeing, I'm going to take a shower. No, you don't," she warned at his motion to follow her. "If you go with me, we'll never get out of this room today."

"If that's a threat, I'll take my chances."

Laughing, Katie pulled out of his grasp. "Later," she said, and with a kiss that promised a private sightseeing tour for later, disappeared into the bathroom, leaving him almost regretting making any plans that included leaving their bed.

Paris. Flowers in every window box, posh little cafés lining cobblestone streets, stylish people bustling to and fro, unforgettable works of art and architecture at every turn, ancient towering cathedrals and historic stone arches, the Seine river meandering through the city, smells of freshly baked pastries and aromas of expensive perfumes wafting through the air—all of it lived up to and exceeded Katie's expectations.

And all of it paled next to the sheer happiness rioting through her because she was with Blake. It felt like a dream, so flawless and wonderful she was afraid to examine it too closely for fear she'd wake and find it couldn't possibly be true.

Hours after they'd started their explorations, Blake stopped at a street corner on a busy intersection and took her hand. "There it is," he said, pointing in the distance to the most gigantic cathedral Katie had ever seen. "Notre Dame."

"Oh, I never imagined… It's amazing."

"Come on." He tugged her and she joined him running across the street to avoid the onslaught of tiny, speeding cars, scooters and bicycles. "I want to get there at sunset."

Just as they approached the entrance to the gothic cathedral, a wedding party began to flood out. They stood aside to watch the spectacle of gorgeously dressed guests, a dozen or so bridesmaids and groomsmen and finally the bride and groom. Blake wrapped an arm around Katie's shoulder and drew her to him.

"She's stunning," she said, captivated by the dark French beauty wrapped in a flowing alabaster gown.

"Not as stunning as you." Lifting her chin with his index finger, he smiled into her eyes.

A warm glow touched Katie's heart and she kissed him sweetly. They stayed there holding each other, exchanging a kiss now and then until the wedding party found their way to the waiting limos and the sun had begun its hazy, saffron descent.

She couldn't help but wonder, as she watched the bride and groom sneak a kiss, if she would ever be that woman in a white flowing gown, married to the man of her dreams. A little sigh escaped her, and she inwardly smiled at her romantic musings. She was with the man of her dreams and she wanted to savor every moment, instead of focusing on what might or might not be.

Resting her head on Blake's shoulder, she turned her thoughts to watching the cathedral transform. Earlier, she'd been awed by the magnitude of the imposing mass of gray towers, huge round stained glass windows, spires, flying buttresses and portals. But now, softened by the glow of the magic hour of dusk, the entire cathedral lit up in reflected gold beauty created one of the most deeply profound visions she had ever seen.

Blake moved to stand behind her, his arms around her waist, his breath close and warm on her neck. "See why I wanted to get here by sunset?"

"Oh, yes, it's unbelievable," she murmured, leaning back into him, mesmerized in thought and vision as together they watched the spectacle of dimming rays of sunlight create magnificent shadows that recalled lifetimes of history, countless loves lost and found, centuries of pain and moments of glorious triumph, all reflected in the unyielding majesty and spiritual prowess of this unequalled monument.

When a shimmering tapestry of changing light encompassed all they could see, church bells began to ring throughout the city, creating a magical fantasia and wrapping them in an ethereal aura of timelessness, Blake gently turned Katie in his arms and backed a step away.

"Blake, what…?"

"I've never been this happy as I have these last two weeks," he said, taking her hand in his. "I don't want it to end once we go back home."

Unexpectedly, he dropped to one knee in front of her and her heart fluttered with surprise and tremulous expectation. He couldn't possibly mean—could he…?

"Katie, I love you," he said, his voice deep and brimming with emotion. "Will you marry me?"

Chapter Seventeen

It was the last thing she'd expected to hear from him today and the single thing she'd wanted to hear for weeks now. "Oh, Blake, I never thought—yes." She looked into his eyes and repeated it, savoring the word and all that went with it. "Yes."

He was on his feet then, sweeping her into his arms, kissing her passionately, mindless of the glances they were getting from passersby. Parting at last, he gently touched her face. "When we get back to Dallas, I want you to pick out an engagement ring," he said. "I have something in mind, one of Penny's designs, but I want it to be your choice."

"I'm sure I'll love it." Stretching up, she kissed him. "I love you."

"Let's celebrate," he said. "I think they may be holding a reservation for us at Chez René."

"Why do I get the feeling you planned this from the moment we got off the plane?" Katie asked as they began walking hand in hand away from the cathedral.

He flashed a smile. "You know me. I don't like to leave anything to chance. I wanted to make it hard for you to say no."

"I wouldn't have said no." And she knew it was true, no matter where and when he'd asked her to marry him.

The rest of their brief stay in France passed in a whirl, with Katie scarcely registering anything of it that didn't directly involve Blake. She didn't have time to think about the implications of the commitment they'd made to each other or the reaction from friends and family. The overwhelming happiness she felt made thinking impossible. Even the flight home, with Dallas growing nearer by the minute, couldn't daunt her joy.

Blake didn't give her any opportunity for contemplation, either. Practically the moment the jet landed, he ushered her into the waiting car and less than an hour later, Katie found herself at the McCord Jewelers flagship store, gazing at the ring Blake had handpicked for her appraisal.

"This," she said, touching a fingertip to a flawless square-cut diamond set in platinum. "This is perfect."

"Then it's yours." Blake picked up the ring and led her back to his office, closing the door against the curious looks and whispers of the store staff before slipping it on her finger. "I promise, no matter what, I'll always love you," he vowed, punctuating it with a tender kiss.

Katie's eyes in turn filled with tears. "Why am I crying again?" she chided herself. "I've never been happier."

"Don't all women cry when they're happy?"

"If you're going to make comparisons—"

"Never. And even if I did, all other women would come up short." He put his arm around her, lightly kissing her temple. "I'm not quite ready to face real life yet. Why don't we put off telling anyone we're home until tomorrow? We can spend tonight alone, deal with everything else in the morning."

"That sounds really nice. Real life is bad enough but facing my parents isn't going to be easy."

Blake frowned a little. "Why? It's not as if you need their permission."

"Of course not," she said. "It's awkward, that's all, so soon after—" She let the sentence die but not quickly enough.

"After Tate, you mean," he said flatly.

"Okay, yes, but it's not only that." Splaying her hands over his chest, she brushed her lips against his. "Let's not worry about all this now. As you said, it'll be easier to deal with in the morning."

She could see he wanted to press the issue, but with a nod he accepted her delaying the inevitable. "How about dinner, then?"

They settled on a small out-of-the-way Japanese restaurant, and to Katie it felt like an extension of the last two weeks. She wanted to convince herself jet lag was responsible for her growing sense of unreality. But in truth, everything had happened so fast and she'd started to question whether or not she'd let herself get caught up the romantic whirlwind that had been San Vincentia and Paris.

"I think I'd better take you home and put you to bed," Blake commented, signaling the waiter for the check. "You look like you're wilting."

"I'm sorry, I guess the jet lag is sinking in.'

"No reason to apologize. You deserve to be tired,

after all the excitement and travelling the past few days."
He reached over and took her hand, his fingers idly
rubbing the ring he'd put on her finger. "Don't worry,"
he said, "everyone will get used to the idea, and if they
don't, to hell with them. All that matters is us."

"You're right," she said softly. "That is all that
matters." And her love for him and the love in his eyes
made it easy to believe.

The next morning, though, waking up in her solitary
bed, her only tangible reminder of the time spent away
her engagement ring, Katie was slammed by doubts. It
had all happened so fast. Had she rushed into her relationship with Blake, heedless of the consequences?

She didn't have answers but told herself she had to
put the questions aside, for at least the day, needing to
concentrate on getting to her office and catching up on
everything that she'd left undone in her absence.

Work, though, didn't turn out to be the distraction
she'd hoped.

Tessa, in the process of handing her several files,
suddenly stopped midgesture, staring wide-eyed at
Katie's left hand. "Oh, my gosh. Is that what I think it is?"

"Yes," Katie said, seeing no point in denying it, though
she would have preferred her and Blake's families had
been the first to know. "Blake and I are engaged."

"I didn't believe it when you kept denying you were
involved, but I never expected…" Tessa stopped, looking a little flustered, and then put on a smile. "Well, congratulations. It looks like you're going to be Mrs.
McCord after all."

Katie flushed at the implication that she'd traded one
McCord man for another, but then hadn't she expected
that reaction? She didn't have time to come up with a

response because her cell rang and she recognized Blake's number. Tessa left with a silently mouthed, "Talk to you later," as Katie picked up the call.

"I'm hoping you can meet me at home this afternoon, say about four?" he said. "I thought we could decide on the best way to tell the families about us."

Tension gripped her but she tried to sound casual, pleased even. "Yes, all right. I should be finished up here by then."

There was a pause and then Blake said, "Is everything all right?"

"It's been a long morning," she hedged. "Tessa managed to pile my desk with paperwork while we were gone and I'm trying to sort through it all."

"If that's all—" He gave her a moment to reply and when she didn't, he said, his voice dropping to that low, husky pitch she'd learned so well, "I miss you. I know it's been less than a day, but I've gotten used to us being together."

"I feel the same way," she said.

She heard a muffled buzz at his end and Blake's exasperated sound. "Damn, I've got another call. I'll see you this afternoon. I love you."

"I love you, too," she murmured.

The way he'd opened up to her, how easily he expressed his feelings to her now, quelled Katie's doubts, at least until the late afternoon, when she was on her way to the McCord mansion. Then, determined to defeat them, she kept reminding herself that they loved each other, and that Blake was right, it didn't matter what anyone else said or thought.

Yet the closer she got to the mansion and Blake, the more she worried it was a battle that her heart wouldn't win.

* * *

Blake met Katie at the front door, stealing a quick kiss, before whisking her out to one back wing of the house, facing the gardens. He'd chosen the Florida room because it was least likely they'd be interrupted there. Closing the expansive sliding glass doors behind them, he turned and drew her to him and kissed her again, this time passionately, telling her with his embrace how long the hours had seemed without her.

When they parted, breathless, he smiled. "Sorry for the cloak-and-dagger entrance, but I wanted us to have time alone before we're discovered. No one ever uses this room, unless my mother has her lady friends for tea."

"It's fine." Gently disengaging herself from his arms, she walked over to stand near the windows, looking out at the landscape that was glazed with the last of the afternoon sun. "You said you wanted to talk."

Something in her tone and the stiff set of her shoulders made him uneasy. He went over to her, putting his hands on her shoulders and gently turning her to face him. "What's bothering you, Katie? And don't tell me it's been a long day or it's jet lag," he said before she could give those excuses again. "I know that's not it."

"Tessa knows we're engaged."

"And that's a bad thing? In a day or two, so will everyone else."

"It's not so much that she knows," Katie said, glancing away from his searching gaze. "It was her reaction. She said it looked like I was going to be Mrs. McCord after all."

"I don't see—"

Katie pulled away from him. "A few months ago I was engaged to your brother. That's what everyone is going to say, that I couldn't have Tate, so I settled for the next best thing."

A cold hard knot settled in his gut. "Is that what you did, Katie, settle for second-best?"

"You know that isn't true."

"Do I? I thought I did. I'd convinced myself that this wasn't about you being on the rebound from Tate. Now, I'm not so sure."

"This has nothing to do with Tate. It never did. I never loved him the way I love you."

"Then what is it about?" Blake gritted out, trying hard to keep a leash on his frustrations.

She looked at him a long moment and he could clearly see the struggle in her eyes to put her feelings to words. "Those weeks in San Vincentia and then Paris," she began, "they were…like a dream. I went there with you, not expecting it to last, and then—everything happened so quickly. I didn't have time to think about what we were doing."

Pacing a few steps away from him, she glanced at his ring on her finger. "I've never loved anyone like this, even Tate. It's so overwhelming that sometimes it feels like it can't be real." Her eyes lifted to his, begging for his understanding. "I never really committed to Tate— I was just raised to believe we were meant for each other. And you've never been in a long-term relationship. I can't help but wonder if either of us knows what we're doing. I'm worried we rushed into this blindly without knowing if what we have is strong enough to last a lifetime."

"You're saying we—you—made a mistake." Blake faced away from her to grip the back of a chair. He couldn't have guessed it would hurt like this, to hear all over again someone telling him—Katie telling him, that once again, he was somebody's mistake.

"Blake—no," she said, the anguish in her voice making him turn to her again, "that's not what I meant. Please, I…I never wanted to hurt you like this, for you to think that I regret loving you. I'm just—" In a jerky abrupt motion, she tugged off her engagement ring, and quickly coming up to him, took his hand and pressed the ring into his palm, closing his fingers around it. "I can't be what you need. You deserve so much better than this."

She spun around and started for the door, her sudden action freezing him in place for several seconds. But the sight of her leaving him spurred him to action and he outpaced her and grasped her wrist, keeping her from walking out of his life.

"Blake…" Tears filled her eyes as she looked at him.

For a moment, he told himself he could let her go, save himself additional grief and heartache by ending it now. It would be the simplest way to resolve things and he nearly made that choice to go back to what he was before, alone, armored against caring, substituting ambition and success for love.

But he couldn't go back. And he'd never before taken the easy way out.

"What do you want, Katie?" he asked. "I can't promise you perfection or that we're never going to have to face any obstacles. I can't stop people from talking. All I can promise is that I'll always love you, and that if you feel the same way, then we will be strong enough."

Opening his hand, he offered her the ring. "Your choice this time. I've made mine."

He held his breath as she searched his eyes and it felt she was searching his heart and soul. After a minute that lasted an eternity, when he'd nearly resigned himself to inevitably losing her, she smiled and held out her left hand.

"Will you put it back on?" she asked softly. "For the last time?"

Blake didn't hesitate. He slid the diamond onto her finger and then pulled her into his arms, sealing their future with a kiss that vowed forever.

Two days later, Blake returned home on a Saturday morning, having spent the past nights with Katie. Her parents were in Austin, celebrating Peter Salgar's recent election as governor, and they had the Salgar estate to themselves. They'd spent their days at their respective offices, but their nights alternated between making love and talking. Today, they planned to begin breaking the news of their engagement, starting at lunch with his family.

First, though, he had some unsettled business with his youngest brother. Katie's insights had made him realize that he was still wrestling with lingering demons and he needed to settle things with Charlie, and his mother, as well. She felt strongly that Blake should be at peace with his family before they could begin thinking about having a family of their own. And he had come, reluctantly at first, finally now, to agree with her, at least where Charlie was concerned.

That was why he'd asked Charlie to come home from college for a weekend to talk. When he saw the wariness written in his little brother's eyes as he stepped into the breakfast room, though, he felt a pang of guilt. His bitterness and anger had caused that look.

Now it was up to him to make it go away.

"Good morning," he said, hoping to ease the tension

with the mundane greeting. "I hope you got a good night's sleep."

"It was fine," Charlie returned with a shrug. "We missed you at dinner last night. Mom said you've been gone a lot lately."

"I'll tell you about that later. Right now, I want to talk about something else. Let's go out back."

There was a chill in the air, and they both pulled on coats. Blake pretended not to notice the sidelong looks Charlie kept slanting at him, knowing his brother was probably confused by his complete turnaround in attitude from the last time they'd met.

"What's on your mind?" Charlie asked when they'd walked a distance from the house.

"A lot. But I'll try to simplify it." He took a breath. "I wanted to apologize."

Charlie looked straight ahead. "For what?"

"For the way I acted when you told me you wanted to meet Rex. For resenting you all these years." Charlie's eyes snapped to him and Blake smiled a little then sobered. "It wasn't fair of me to blame you for what happened between Mom and Rex and my father all those years ago."

"It wasn't fair the way Mom treated you," Charlie muttered. He shifted his shoulders, staring at the ground. "I felt guilty for always being her favorite. I never knew why, which just made it worse."

"None of it was your fault. I think it's time we both put it behind us." He laid a hand on Charlie's shoulder. "You're a great guy and you deserve the love of both your parents. I hope you can get to know your father. You both deserve a chance to make up for lost time."

"Thanks, Blake, really, this means more to me than I can tell you. I never expected this from you." He paused then added, "Rex and I are making headway. It's weird, but we have a connection."

"You'll always be a McCord, too. I hope you remember that." Reaching out, he pulled his brother into a hug, for the first time he could remember since Charlie was a child. Charlie returned the embrace and when they backed away, Blake pushed a hand through his hair, clearing his throat against the lump there.

Yet he suddenly felt lighter, the heaviness of guilt and resentment receding, replaced with a warmth and closeness he'd missed between him and Charlie.

"So are you going to tell me what the big secret is?" Charlie asked as they started walking back toward the house.

"Big secret?"

"Come on, Blake. You disappear for a couple of weeks and when you do get back home, nobody can find you. And coincidentally, no one's seen Katie in all that time, either."

Blake smiled at Charlie's not so subtle probing. "Looks like you get to be the first to know—Katie and I are engaged."

"Engaged? Seriously? That's great!"

"You think so?"

"Why wouldn't I?" Charlie asked. "I never thought she and Tate were right for each other even though everybody kept pushing them together. What, are you worried about what Mom's going to say?"

"It doesn't matter what she or anyone else says. We love each other and that's not going to change. So—are you going to join us for lunch and take our side when we make the big announcement to everyone else?"

Charlie flashed him a grin. "I wouldn't miss it."

* * *

Katie sat next to Blake that afternoon, trying not to let her face give away the riotous happiness that threatened to burst out. Eleanor, Tate, Tanya and Charlie had joined them and Katie could see it was all Charlie could do not to burst out grinning.

Blake reached for her hand under the table, brushing his thumb over her fingers. Inwardly she smiled, feeling both joyous and nervous, sure there would be mixed reactions, also knowing she no longer cared.

All that truly mattered to her now was that her fiancé sat next to her, her hand in his, his ring a symbol of their love and the commitment they had made to each other for the rest of their lives. She had, for the first time in her life, made her choice, and it was Blake.

They were nearly finished with lunch when Eleanor put down her glass and looked pointedly at Blake and Katie. "This has been nice, but it's not like you, Blake, to arrange a family meeting without some purpose. Are you going to tell us?"

Exchanging a glance with him, Katie let him bring their clasped hands into view, drawing everyone's attention to brilliant diamond on her hand.

"Katie and I are getting married," he said simply.

There was a brief silence in which Eleanor stared and Tate frowned, while Tanya and Charlie broke out in smiles.

"We love each other," Katie said softly, looking directly at Eleanor. "I know you can understand that."

They shared a moment when Katie felt Eleanor weighing the sincerity of Katie's declaration and then Eleanor nodded. "I do understand."

"Is this what you want?" Tate asked.

Blake tensed, but Katie squeezed his hand and smiled at Tate. "It's everything I want."

"Then, congratulations," Tate said, his expression lighter. He lifted his glass and the others followed suit, though Eleanor was the last. "May you be as happy as Tanya and I are."

Katie's gaze went to Blake and he focused only on her and promised, "We will be."

Heedless of their audience, this time it was she that drew him into a kiss, knowing without doubt that with Blake, she'd truly found forever.

* * * * *

*Celebrate 60 years of pure reading pleasure
with Harlequin®!*

To commemorate the event, Silhouette Special
Edition invites you to Ashley O'Ballivan's bed-
and-breakfast in the small town of Stone Creek.
The beautiful innkeeper will have her hands full
caring for her old flame Jack McCall. He's on the
run and recovering from a mysterious illness, but
that won't stop him from trying to win Ashley back.

*Enjoy an exclusive glimpse of Linda Lael Miller's
AT HOME IN STONE CREEK
Available in November 2009
from Silhouette Special Edition®*

The helicopter swung abruptly sideways in a dizzying arch, setting Jack McCall's fever-ravaged brain spinning.

His friend's voice sounded tinny, coming through the earphones. "You belong in a hospital," he said. "Not some backwater bed-and-breakfast."

All Jack really knew about the virus raging through his system was that it wasn't contagious, and there was no known treatment for it besides a lot of rest and quiet. "I don't like hospitals," he responded, hoping he sounded like his normal self. "They're full of sick people."

Vince Griffin chuckled but it was a dry sound, rough at the edges. "What's in Stone Creek, Arizona?" he asked. "Besides a whole lot of nothin'?"

Ashley O'Ballivan was in Stone Creek, and she was a whole lot of somethin', but Jack had neither the strength nor the inclination to explain. After the way he'd ducked out six months before, he didn't expect a welcome, knew he didn't deserve one. But Ashley, being Ashley, would take him in whatever her misgivings.

He had to get to Ashley; he'd be all right.

He closed his eyes, letting the fever swallow him.

There was no telling how much time had passed when he became aware of the chopper blades slowing overhead. Dimly, he saw the private ambulance waiting on the airfield outside of Stone Creek; it seemed that twilight had descended.

Jack sighed with relief. His clothes felt clammy against his flesh. His teeth began to chatter as two figures unloaded a gurney from the back of the ambulance and waited for the blades to stop.

"Great," Vince remarked, unsnapping his seat belt. "Those two look like volunteers, not real EMTs."

The chopper bounced sickeningly on its runners, and Vince, with a shake of his head, pushed open his door and jumped to the ground, head down.

Jack waited, wondering if he'd be able to stand on his own. After fumbling unsuccessfully with the buckle on his seat belt, he decided not.

When it was safe the EMTs approached, following Vince, who opened Jack's door.

His old friend Tanner Quinn stepped around Vince, his grin not quite reaching his eyes.

"You look like hell warmed over," he told Jack cheerfully.

"Since when are you an EMT?" Jack retorted.

Tanner reached in, wedged a shoulder under Jack's right arm and hauled him out of the chopper. His knees immediately buckled, and Vince stepped up, supporting him on the other side.

"In a place like Stone Creek," Tanner replied, "everybody helps out."

They reached the wheeled gurney, and Jack found himself on his back.

Tanner and the second man strapped him down, a process that brought back a few bad memories.

"Is there even a hospital in this place?" Vince asked irritably from somewhere in the night.

"There's a pretty good clinic over in Indian Rock," Tanner answered easily, "and it isn't far to Flagstaff." He paused to help his buddy hoist Jack and the gurney into the back of the ambulance. "You're in good hands, Jack. My wife is the best veterinarian in the state."

Jack laughed raggedly at that.

Vince muttered a curse.

Tanner climbed into the back beside him, perched on some kind of fold-down seat. The other man shut the doors.

"You in any pain?" Tanner said as his partner climbed into the driver's seat and started the engine.

"No." Jack looked up at his oldest and closest friend and wished he'd listened to Vince. Ever since he'd come down with the virus—a week after snatching a five-year-old girl back from her non-custodial parent, a small-time Colombian drug dealer—he hadn't been able to think about anyone or anything but Ashley. When he *could* think, anyway.

Now, in one of the first clearheaded moments he'd experienced since checking himself out of Bethesda the day before, he realized he might be making a major mistake. Not by facing Ashley—he owed her that much and a lot more. No, he could be putting her in danger, putting Tanner and his daughter and his pregnant wife in danger, too.

"I shouldn't have come here," he said, keeping his voice low.

Tanner shook his head, his jaw clamped down hard as though he was irritated by Jack's statement.

"This is where you belong," Tanner insisted. "If you'd had sense enough to know that six months ago, old buddy, when you bailed on Ashley without so much as a fare-thee-well, you wouldn't be in this mess."

Ashley. The name had run through his mind a million times in those six months, but hearing somebody say it out loud was like having a fist close around his insides and squeeze hard.

Jack couldn't speak.

Tanner didn't press for further conversation.

The ambulance bumped over country roads, finally hitting smooth blacktop.

"Here we are," Tanner said. "Ashley's place."

* * * * *

Will Jack be able to patch things up with Ashley,
or will his past put the woman he loves
in harm's way?
Find out in
AT HOME IN STONE CREEK
by Linda Lael Miller
Available November 2009
from Silhouette Special Edition®

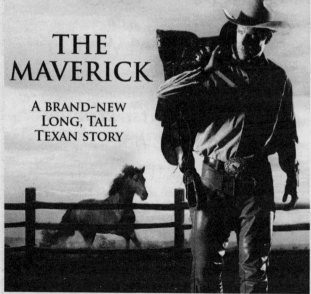

Silhouette Desire

FROM *NEW YORK TIMES* BESTSELLING AUTHOR

DIANA PALMER

THE MAVERICK

A BRAND-NEW LONG, TALL TEXAN STORY

HARLEQUIN *Romance*

This November,
queen of the rugged rancher

PATRICIA THAYER

teams up with

DONNA ALWARD

to bring you an extra-special treat
this holiday season—

two romantic stories
in one book!

Join sisters Amelia and Kelley for Christmas at
Rocking H Ranch where these feisty cowgirls swap
presents for proposals, mistletoe for marriage and
experience the unbeatable rush of falling in love!

Available in November wherever books are sold.

www.eHarlequin.com

HRI7619

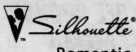

Romantic
SUSPENSE

Blackout At Christmas

Beth Cornelison,
Sharron McClellan,
Jennifer Morey

What happens when a major blackout shuts
down the entire Western seaboard on Christmas
Eve? Follow stories of danger, intrigue and
romance as three women learn to trust their
instincts to survive and open their hearts to the
love that unexpectedly comes their way.

*Available November
wherever books are sold.*

Visit Silhouette Books at www.eHarlequin.com

SRS27653

REQUEST YOUR FREE BOOKS!

2 FREE NOVELS PLUS 2 FREE GIFTS!

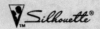

SPECIAL EDITION®

Life, Love and Family!

YES! Please send me 2 FREE Silhouette Special Edition® novels and my 2 FREE gifts (gifts are worth about $10). After receiving them, if I don't wish to receive any more books, I can return the shipping statement marked "cancel." If I don't cancel, I will receive 6 brand-new novels every month and be billed just $4.24 per book in the U.S. or $4.99 per book in Canada. That's a savings of at least 15% off the cover price! It's quite a bargain! Shipping and handling is just 50¢ per book.* I understand that accepting the 2 free books and gifts places me under no obligation to buy anything. I can always return a shipment and cancel at any time. Even if I never buy another book from Silhouette, the two free books and gifts are mine to keep forever.

235 SDN EYN4 335 SDN EYPG

Name	(PLEASE PRINT)	
Address		Apt. #
City	State/Prov.	Zip/Postal Code

Signature (if under 18, a parent or guardian must sign)

Mail to the Silhouette Reader Service:
IN U.S.A.: P.O. Box 1867, Buffalo, NY 14240-1867
IN CANADA: P.O. Box 609, Fort Erie, Ontario L2A 5X3

Not valid to current subscribers of Silhouette Special Edition books.

Want to try two free books from another line?
Call 1-800-873-8635 or visit www.morefreebooks.com.

* Terms and prices subject to change without notice. Prices do not include applicable taxes. Sales tax applicable in N.Y. Canadian residents will be charged applicable provincial taxes and GST. Offer not valid in Quebec. This offer is limited to one order per household. All orders subject to approval. Credit or debit balances in a customer's account(s) may be offset by any other outstanding balance owed by or to the customer. Please allow 4 to 6 weeks for delivery. Offer available while quantities last.

Your Privacy: Silhouette is committed to protecting your privacy. Our Privacy Policy is available online at www.eHarlequin.com or upon request from the Reader Service. From time to time we make our lists of customers available to reputable third parties who may have a product or service of interest to you. If you would prefer we not share your name and address, please check here. ☐

SSE09R

Stay up-to-date on all your romance-reading news with the brand-new Harlequin *Inside Romance!*

The Harlequin *Inside Romance* is a **FREE** quarterly newsletter highlighting our upcoming series releases and promotions!

Click on the *Inside Romance* **link on the front page of www.eHarlequin.com or e-mail us at InsideRomance@Harlequin.ca to sign up to receive your FREE newsletter today!**

COMING NEXT MONTH

Available October 27, 2009

#2005 AT HOME IN STONE CREEK—Linda Lael Miller
Sometimes Ashley O'Ballivan felt like the only single woman left in Stone Creek. All because of security expert Jack McCall—the man who broke her heart years ago. Now Jack was mysteriously back in town…and Ashley's single days were numbered.

#2006 A LAWMAN FOR CHRISTMAS—Marie Ferrarella
Kate's Boys
When a car accident landed her mother in the hospital, it was Kelsey Marlowe's worst nightmare. Luckily, policeman Morgan Donnelly was there to save her mom, and the nightmare turned into a dream come true—as Kelsey fell hard for the sexy lawman!

#2007 QUINN McCLOUD'S CHRISTMAS BRIDE—Lois Faye Dyer
The McClouds of Montana
Wolf Creek's temporary sheriff Quinn McCloud was a wanderer; librarian Abigail Foster was the type to set down roots. But when they joined forces to help a little girl left on Abigail's doorstep, did opposites ever attract! And just in time for a Christmas wedding.

#2008 THE TEXAN'S DIAMOND BRIDE—Teresa Hill
The Foleys and the McCords
When Travis Foley caught gemologist Paige McCord snooping around on his property for the fabled Santa Magdalena Diamond, it spelled trouble for the feuding families. But what was it about this irresistible interloper that gave the rugged rancher pause?

#2009 MERRY CHRISTMAS, COWBOY!—Cindy Kirk
Meet Me in Montana
All academic Lauren Van Meveren wanted from her trip to Big Sky country was peace and quiet to write her dissertation. But when she moved onto widower Seth Anderssen's ranch to help with his daughter, Lauren got the greatest gift of all—true love.

#2010 MOONLIGHT AND MISTLETOE—Dawn Temple
When her estranged father sent Beverly Hills attorney Kyle Anderson to strong-arm her into a settlement, Shayna Miller was determined to resist…until Kyle melted her heart and had her heading for the nearest mistletoe, head-over-heels in love….